PLAYING OFFSIDES

WYNCOTE WOLVES
BOOK THREE

CALI MELLE

Cover Designer: Cat Imb, TRC Designs

Editor: Rumi Khan

Sometimes love will find you in the most unexpected places...

CHAPTER ONE
CAMERON

"Sawyer!" Coach calls my name as he ducks his head from his office. We all just arrived for practice, but judging by the look on his face, he isn't too happy to see me right now. "In my office, now."

Swallowing hard, I nod and prop my stick up next to my bag. Logan and August both look over at me, eyebrows raised in suspicion. Shrugging at them, I turn to head toward his office, with an idea of what this is about.

Hayden King walks past me, his eyebrows drawn together. "What'd you do, Cam?"

Ignoring him, I keep moving toward our coach's office. I don't have time to give anyone an explanation, especially with so much hanging on the line.

My entire life of playing hockey could be in jeopardy after this talk we're about to have.

As I step into his office, he motions for me to sit down as he takes his seat at his desk. His expression is impassive, with a hint of disappointment lingering in his hazel eyes. Staring back at him, I notice the wrinkles on his face and the specks of gray in his dark hair.

"I'm imagining you probably have an idea of why I wanted to talk to you, Cameron," he starts, folding his hands on his desk in front of him. He frowns slightly as I nod. "I was notified that your biology grade dropped below a C. As you are aware, we require that you have at least a seventy-five percent in all of your classes to remain on the team."

"Yes, sir," I reply, nodding as my stomach sinks. "I've been struggling with that class, and my grade just recently dropped after a recent exam I bombed."

"With the regional championship coming up soon, you're going to need to bring your grade up and maintain it in order to be able to play." He pauses for a moment, the frown still fixed to his lips. "Are you aware that the grade requirements also apply to your scholarship?"

Swallowing roughly, I nod again. "Yes, I'm aware

of that. If I am able to bring my grade back up, will it affect my scholarship then?"

Coach shakes his head. "As long as you can get your grade back up to where we need it, you are able to play and your scholarship will remain unaffected." He pauses for a moment, pursing his lips. "Have you considered possibly finding a tutor?"

"I've been trying to study myself, but the thought has crossed my mind, since what I'm doing obviously isn't working."

"Look into your options because we're cutting it pretty close, and I would hate to see you lose any game time this late in the season." His eyes bounce back and forth between mine. "You're an asset to this team, Cameron. And you are on your way to big things in the future. The last thing I want to see is for those opportunities to vanish for you."

My stomach rolls as the realization of my reality strikes me. I've worked so hard for so long for this to all go away. As a kid, I grew up living and breathing hockey. It has always been my life, the one thing I had devoted all of my time and energy to. I can't afford to lose it all this late in life.

Since I'm in my junior year of college, I literally have to make it through next year and then hopefully get drafted into the NHL. That has always been the goal and I refuse to give that up now. My mother always told me to dream big and shoot past the stars. I took that to heart and shot past the damn universe.

"I will bring my grade up, Coach. I promise you that it won't come in the way of me being able to play."

"I hope so, Cameron," he says as he rises to his feet and motions toward the door. "Go get ready for practice. And be ready to skate your ass off out there."

Nodding, I rise to my feet and head toward the door. "Thanks, Coach. For giving me the opportunity to bring my grade up, rather than just booting me from the team now."

"You're a good kid, Sawyer. And one hell of a player. I'd be a fool to let you go now."

His words snake their way around my heart, clutching it hard. Compliments aren't something we typically get from him, so hearing his praise has me feeling like I'm walking on top of the world right now. I know I don't come close to playing like August or Logan, but I play my position pretty damn well.

Now, all I need to do is make sure I can get my biology grade up and not completely fuck this up.

As I walk back out into the locker room, I watch the last of the guys heading out, laughing about something as they give each other shit. A smile doesn't come close to touching my lips as a heaviness rests on my shoulders. None of them have to worry about this shit like I do. As of right now, I'm the only one on the team here who is on a scholarship because I literally cannot afford to be here.

Some of the other guys got here on full-rides too, but most of them come from money, so paying for their schooling without it wouldn't be a problem. I come from a family where both of my parents worked their asses off just to be able to scrape up the spare funds to put me through all of the financial demands with hockey.

I owe them my life and when I make it big, my first goal is to pay them back for everything they've done for me.

If I were to fuck this up now and lose my scholarship, it would definitely be a slap in the face to them. Not to mention the fact that I'm the first in our family to make it to college. High school was hard as hell for me, but I made it through with impeccable grades. I owe it to Logan and August for helping me whenever things got rough.

There's just too much riding on what I have

going right now, but I can't think about that now. It's time to get out on the ice and practice. These guys are like my family and the last thing I'm going to do is let them down too.

Pushing the lingering thoughts from my mind, I quickly get dressed, strapping on all of my pads before pulling on my practice jersey. It doesn't take long for me to lace my skates, making sure they are as tight as I can get them before I slide my helmet onto my head. Grabbing my gloves and my stick, I head through the locker room and step into the tunnel that leads to the arena.

Standing at the edge of the ice, I watch as they all skate around effortlessly, taking practice shots with Asher, our goaltender. I can't help but feel a twinge of guilt, knowing that I could end up letting them all down. None of them know in this moment and I don't know if I'm ready to tell any of them. I know they would offer nothing but support, but it almost feels shameful.

My skates hit the ice and I push off with my feet, feeling the muscles tighten in my thighs, before gliding toward my teammates. Logan and August slide over to me, their skates slashing through the ice as they abruptly stop near me.

"Everything good?" Logan asks, his eyes

searching mine through the cage covering his face. August stares back at me, waiting for some response before offering any words of his own.

"Yeah," I lie through my teeth, not yet ready to discuss my problem with either of them. The two of them are my closest friends and I can't stand the thought of disappointing them in this moment.

Hayden skates over to us too, curiosity written all over his expression. "Coach chew your ass out for something?"

"Something like that," I mumble, forcing out a laugh to brush off the awkwardness.

Hayden smirks at me, his arrogance rolling off him in waves. "Trust me. Compared to the shit I pulled at my last school, I'm sure you're not in nearly as much trouble."

"I mean, he didn't sleep with the coach's daughter like you did, King," August reminds him as he rolls his eyes. "Has anyone told you that it was a dumb-ass move, by the way?"

Logan laughs and Hayden glares at August.

"I mean, it seemed like a good idea at the time," Hayden shrugs, his expression softening. "It's a mistake I don't plan on repeating again, though."

"That's probably a good idea," I laugh, slapping the puck away from his stick. Being around them has the ability to lift my mood, but the reminder of my reality still lingers in the back of my mind. "Let's go," I tell the three of them, skating off in the direction of the puck.

Sometimes, hockey is the only thing that can clear my mind of the bad shit.

And maybe it's because it is all I've ever had.

CHAPTER TWO
ASPEN

Glancing up at the clock on the wall, I watch as the hands continue ticking, counting down the time until class starts. Call it a nervous habit, but I'm always in the room at least ten minutes before my first lecture starts. I've never been late a day in my life and it's because I can't afford to miss a single second of being here.

Wyncote University was literally the most random college that I could have chosen. Coming from the West Coast, I never saw anything outside of California until I moved away for school. I never felt the snow or the coldness on my skin. Only the warmth and the salty, ocean air.

I would be lying if I said that I didn't miss it. The

ocean was the one place that I felt at peace, even though it was something that could easily end my life in one swift sweep of its angry waves. My mother inherited the house that we lived in and it was right along the coast, with the beach in our backyard.

It was weird that we never traveled, considering the fact that my family was well off, but as I got older, it all made sense. My father was always taking his business trips, but we were never invited along because his extra seat was already saved for his assistant. I was fifteen when I found out about their long-standing affair. I had just been diagnosed with ADHD at the time and was struggling with balancing medications. Finding out about the affair did not help my stress levels.

My mother knew of it, but she was locked into his financial security, so she never bothered to challenge him on it. She grew up poor in the city with a single mom. She wasn't going to jeopardize what she had in life just because my father was too busy with other women. As long as we were provided for, my mother didn't care.

That didn't stop her from developing severe anxiety. It was almost as if she were afraid to leave our home in fear that my father would take it all away from us. He was never a malicious man, despite their marital issues. His career was always more important than family time, though, hence why I had never been outside of California's state lines.

When it was time for me to go to college, my parents were thrilled when I wanted to study medicine. My father tried to map out my entire life, picking a school for me that would offer the best pre-med courses. Wyncote University wasn't on that list, so I made sure that it was the one that I picked.

It was still a prestigious and decent school, but it wasn't the one my father wanted, so that made it even more appealing. The fact that it was in Vermont was even more ideal. Being as far away from the toxicity that lived in the walls of our home was something I needed. Coming here was like a breath of fresh air.

It was an adjustment, but I've been here for two years now and have settled in with a life of my own. When it comes down to it, my studies always come first. I don't care much to partake in the partying that some of my friends indulge in. A drink or two is enough for me before I'm ready to crawl into bed with a good book.

As I arrange my things on the table in front of

me, other students begin to file into the classroom. Soon, most of the seats are filled, except for the one to my left. Glancing over to my right, I smile as Delilah sits down next to me. I met her my freshman year and we've been friends since then. She's studying pre-med too, but she has a little more of a wild streak than I do.

Delilah yawns as she drops her head onto the desk. "I wanna go back to bed."

Laughing lightly, I shake my head at her. "Late night?"

She lifts her head, nodding. "I ended up going to that party I was telling you about. You were smart to stay home because I am so hungover right now."

"Yeah, I can't say that I envy you."

"One of these days, I'm forcing you to come along and you're going to actually get drunk," she tells me, her bright blue eyes searching mine. "And don't even try and tell me that it's happened before. At most, I've seen you get a buzz. You need to have at least one drunken night during your college years and I hate to break it to you, babe, but you're running out of time."

My eyebrows tug together as I scrunch my face at her. "Hardly. We still have two more years and then med school too... so I will have plenty of opportunities for it to happen."

"Come on, Aspen," she groans, propping her elbow on the table as she drops her hand down to it. "You know that I am all for taking school seriously, but don't you think that you take it *too* seriously sometimes?"

I shrug, feeling uncomfortable under her gaze. "I don't know. Maybe."

There's movement to the other side of me and I glance over, noticing as Cameron Sawyer takes a seat next to me. My eyes widen slightly, my heart pounding in my chest. I've had different classes with Cam since freshman year, but we've never had a single conversation. And he's never taken the empty seat next to me.

"Aspen," Delilah nudges me as I look back at her, quickly recovering from my shock. "You need to lighten up a little bit."

"I'll try," I tell her, honestly meaning the words as I speak them. I don't try to be uptight, but she is right about taking school seriously. It's mainly because I don't want to live like my mother did. I want to be able to provide for myself and not need someone else. Self-reliance is my ultimate goal.

The professor walks in front of the class as she

begins to scribble some things on the board, diving directly into what we're currently learning in biology. Grabbing my notebook, I flip it open to a fresh page and stare directly ahead, listening intently as she begins to go over new material.

Delilah follows suit and I see her out of the corner of my eye, jotting down notes of her own. She might be more of party girl than me, but when it comes down to it, she's here for the same reasons I am and I know she isn't going to risk messing any of that up. Most of the students here in pre-med are relatively serious about their studies.

Glancing to the other side, I notice Cam not writing anything down with his gaze fixed on the side of my face instead of at the board at the front of the class. Swallowing hard, I attempt to ignore him as I focus on our professor's voice and the words she speaks. But I can't shake the unsettling feeling, knowing I'm pinned under his gaze right now.

Tearing my eyes away from my notes, my gaze slices to his. "What?" I whisper, my voice harsh as I stare back at him.

"Can we talk after class?"

My face contours and my grip tightens around my pen as my stomach flutters. I stare back into Cameron's dark green eyes, fighting the urge to scan his features. I've studied him over the years and God was good to him when he sculpted his face, like a perfectly chiseled sculpture. "About what?"

There is absolutely nothing that Cameron Sawyer and I would have to talk about. We live two completely different lives. He's one of the hockey team's star players and I'm the nerdy, pre-med student. Cam is always hanging with his friends, hitting up all the parties, while I'm tucked away in my apartment with my nose shoved in a book.

We're polar freaking opposites. And not to mention, we've never had a single conversation so we are nowhere close to even being friends.

"I need your help with something," he says quietly, his voice only to be heard by me. My heart races as the sound slides like silk over my eardrums. "But no one can know."

The butterflies in my stomach flutter their wings, scratching against the inside of my stomach as I tear my gaze away from his and look back to the board. I attempt to focus on the professor and begin writing my notes again when I still feel Cam's gaze on the side of my face.

I try to ignore it until I can't anymore.

"So, is that a yes or a no?"

Whipping my head to the side, I cut my eyes to him. "If I say yes, will you shut up?"

A smirk forms on his lips, his bright eyes shining back at me. "Yes."

"Is there something you would like to share with the class, Miss Rossi?" the professor calls out, her eyes pinned on mine. Abruptly glancing at her, I all but shrink under her gaze as I shake my head. "Very well," she nods. "Please keep it down because some of the students are trying to hear what I'm actually saying."

"Sorry," I apologize, my voice sounding as small as I feel. A heat creeps up my neck, rapidly spreading across my cheeks as I drop my gaze back down to my notes in front of me as everyone's wandering gazes look back to our professor.

Delilah glances over at me and I look up at her as she raises an eyebrow. She doesn't dare utter a single word, but I know that I'll be interrogated by her later. Especially after the way her eyes look past me to Cam, widening slightly before her gaze meets mine again. A ghost of a smile plays on her lips and I roll my eyes at her.

"You didn't give me an answer," Cam whispers, leaning close enough to me that the smell of his cologne overwhelms my senses.

Oh my god, he is relentless. And he smells so good.

"Yes. Now shut the hell up," I growl at him, my voice barely audible.

Cam chuckles lightly, finally pulling out his own notebook and pen as he begins to listen along to the lecture. He leaves me feeling unsettled and unable to focus on a single thing happening at the front of the room. All I can focus on is the lingering smell of his cologne and the sound of his voice rattling inside my brain.

Class ends sooner than I realize and for the first time ever, I'm practically the first one exiting the room. Leaving Delilah behind, I rush out into the hallway, looking for somewhere to hide—somewhere to catch my breath. I know I'll see her later in the day and will have to answer for my unusual behavior.

I'm barely down the hall when I hear his voice and my name rolling off his tongue like that's exactly where it belongs.

"Aspen!" Cam calls out after me, hot on my heels as he jogs in my direction. "Wait up!"

A defeated sigh escapes me when I realize that there's no possible way to escape him. Instead, my only option is to face him head-on and see what exactly it is he wants. Slowly turning around, I cross my arms over my chest as Cam comes to a halt in front of me.

His cheeks are flushed and his chest rises and falls with each rapid breath that he takes.

"What do you want, Cameron?" I question him, my tone clipped as I tilt my head to the side.

"Can we talk somewhere a little more..." He pauses for a moment, glancing around the hallway nervously as students shuffle past us. "Private?"

Shaking my head, I stand my ground. "Here is good."

Cameron's throat bobs as he swallows hard and nods. There's a nervousness about him, something I can't quite put my finger on. He usually exudes confidence, but with the way he's running his hand through his hair right now, he looks anything but. He's flustered as hell, shifting his weight on his feet.

"I need your help."

CHAPTER THREE
CAMERON

Aspen gives me a blank stare. "Yeah, you've already said that."

Her indifference is unexpected. I don't really know her, but from what I've observed, Aspen is usually quiet and more reserved. Mouse-like, if you will. I've only really seen her with Delilah or a few of the other girls that hang out in their group.

Even though we've never shared an encounter before, there's something about Aspen that is hard to ignore. She's an enigma—a mystery. Her eyes are a soft sage color, her cheekbones high and prominent. My eyes travel down the curve of her slender neck as she grabs her raven-colored hair and swings it over her shoulder in an effort to shield herself from my wandering eye.

Lifting my gaze, I meet her look of indifference again. Her plump lips part slightly, her tongue darting out to wet them before she speaks again. "We've attended the same university for the past two years, have been classmates in numerous classes, and this is the first time that we're having a conversation." She pauses for a moment, her eyes narrowing at me. "Why the hell should I help you?"

There's a harshness in her tone, though it doesn't take away from the sultry lilt of her voice. The corners of my lips attempt to curl upward, but I don't allow the smirk to form as she stares at me expectantly, waiting for a response.

"I mean, you've never tried to talk to me before, either."

A harsh laugh falls from her lips as she shakes her head at me. "What could we possibly have to talk about? We literally have nothing in common, Cam. We live in two separate worlds."

"How do you know that? Get to know me and let me change your mind."

Aspen snorts, rolling her eyes. "Yeah, hard pass. I have to get to class, it was nice talking to you, Cameron."

My face contorts, my heart pounding in my chest as I watch her spin on her heel and begin to walk the other way. She has such a distaste for me and I'm confused by it, but obviously my charm isn't going to work on her.

Jogging after her, I grab her arm, spinning her back around. "Aspen, please," I practically beg, my eyes desperately searching hers. "I'm desperate here."

A sigh slips from her lips and she purses them. "What do you need help with?"

Wrapping my hand around her wrist, I pull her over to the wall, away from listening ears. "I'm about to fail biology and I need a tutor to help me get my grade up. My scholarship and game time are on the line with this one."

Realization passes through her eyes and she frowns. "And that's why you said no one can know. You don't want anyone to know about your current status with your academic standing."

"Exactly."

Aspen stares back at me for a moment, chewing on the inside of her cheek as she considers my plea. A soft sigh slips from her lips as her shoulders sag in defeat. "Fine, I will help you."

I'm caught off guard by her actually agreeing. I

don't have anything to offer her in return for the favor, but I have to come up with something. Surely, she can't expect to do it for free.

"What can I do to pay you back? I can't have you doing a huge favor for me like this without me returning it in some way," I tell her, feeling my pride quickly dissolving. Asking for help was hard enough for me to do, and now I can't help but feel uncomfortable with the entire situation.

How am I supposed to tell her that I don't have the extra money to pay her? With my demanding schedule with hockey and classes, I don't have the time to work a part-time job. I'm literally here on a full-ride scholarship and any extra money that I have is what my parents send me to help me pay for anything I may need.

The last thing I want to do is ask them for more money to pay for my tutoring. By doing that, I'm opening the door for disappointment—for them to see that I'm potentially going to fuck everything up.

Aspen tilts her head to the side, her eyebrows drawing together. "I don't need anything in return, Cam." Her voice is soft as her eyes search mine. "Consider it a favor I'm doing out of the kindness of my heart. Plus, it's something I can add to my college résumé."

"If you do this for me, I will be in your debt forever," I breathe, feeling relief flood me, as well as the shame of being in this position. "Seriously, I will pay you back somehow, okay?"

She shakes her head. "You don't owe me anything, Cameron."

"If you can help me get out of this damn mess, I owe you everything." Pausing for a moment, I drop my voice lower, so only she can hear me. "Can you just promise me that you won't tell anyone about this arrangement?"

The corners of her lips curl upward and she nods. "Your secret is safe with me."

A smile consumes my mouth and I stare down into her sage eyes. "Thank you, Aspen. I know we don't really know each other and this is kind of out of nowhere. So, seriously... thank you."

"Thank me after we get your grade back up." She adjusts her bag on her shoulder, glancing at the time on her phone. "I do need to get to my next class, though. Let me give you my number and we can figure out when we can fit some study sessions into your schedule."

Nodding, I pull out my phone and Aspen tells me her number as I enter it and save it. Pressing on the Call button, she stares at her screen as it lights up and declines the call as she glances up at me with an eyebrow raised.

"In case you need my number before I text you," I tell her with a shrug, watching as a pink hue spreads across her cheeks.

Aspen clears her throat, shifting her weight nervously on her feet as she tucks her phone back into the side pocket of her bag. "I have to get to class, but if I don't hear from you this evening, I'll text you."

"Perfect," I smile at her as she spins on her heel and heads down the hall in the direction of her next class. Leaning against the wall, I shove my hands into the pockets of my joggers and watch her until she disappears from my sight.

This might be the lowest point in my college years, but I'm hopeful for what is to come from working with Aspen. She's exactly what I need in my life right now... I just hope I don't find a way to fuck this up too.

CHAPTER FOUR
ASPEN

The rest of the day feels like I'm caught in a weird time warp. All of my classes feel like they drag on forever, but before I know it, the day is over and I'm heading back to my apartment. I live in a studio apartment by myself and it's more than enough space for me. When I first decided to move here instead of traveling home every break and during the summer, my mother wasn't exactly thrilled.

One of the things she insisted was that I get an apartment with a friend or something, or at least a one-bedroom place. But the space I live in is plenty for me. I don't bring people over to entertain. I literally just need enough room to have a bed, kitchen, and a bathroom. And that's even being modest, because for a studio, it's pretty freaking big

After grabbing something to eat from the café around the corner, I come back to my apartment and sit down to study. And just like earlier in the day, I'm more distracted than I've ever been. I can't focus for shit on my studies and I don't need that to happen and mess up my perfect GPA.

I glance over at the cabinet above the sink. It's where I keep my ADHD meds. I usually only take them in the morning and around lunchtime. If I took another one now, it could potentially help get my mind back on track. A sigh slips from my lips as I hang my head in defeat. Who am I kidding? It might help me focus, but I'll be focusing on the wrong things.

I haven't been able to get my interaction with Cam out of my mind and the way that he looked so desperate asking me for help. Because the university I attend caters to our hockey team, everyone knows who all of the players are. They're practically like celebrities, almost as if they own the damn place when they walk around.

Everyone knows Cameron Sawyer, and like I told him, we've had classes together the past two years and never spoke a word before today. Our lives are entirely different, but this isn't an arrangement for us to be friends. Neither of us ever said anything about being friends.

I wouldn't say I dislike him, because that would mean I know him well enough to make a judgment like that. Everything I've heard about him is your run-of-the-mill cliché jock stuff. He's known as the life of the party and a little bit of a playboy who never maintains anything serious with any of the girls he messes around with.

If there's one thing Cam made clear today, it's that hockey is his entire life and he can't afford to put any of that in jeopardy. And right now, *all* of that is in jeopardy.

I don't know why I agreed to help him, but with the way he was looking at me, it was virtually impossible to say no to him. Plus, I was always taught to treat others the way that you want to be treated. He caught me off guard at first, which prompted my walls to go up. This isn't my first time tutoring someone and it's hard to not feel like someone is using you.

And in a way, he is. I'm completely in agreement with the situation because I don't want to see him fail. He seems like a good enough guy. He's dependent upon his scholarship or he wouldn't be so worried about keeping his academics in good standing like he is. As much as I don't know him, I can't help but root for him and want to see him succeed.

If I can be someone who helps him along his journey, then so be it. If the universe didn't intend on it happening that way, Cam never would have approached me about it. He needs my help and I feel compelled to give it to him.

Perhaps it's a way that I can build some good karma for myself too. Give to the world what you want to receive. I don't know if any of that stuff really holds any weight, but what can it hurt?

Taking a break from my studying, I check my phone and notice there's still nothing from Cam. I don't know his schedule or if he had practice tonight, but it's already after nine o'clock at night. He asked me to text him if I didn't hear from him first, so here goes nothing.

ASPEN

Hey Cameron, it's Aspen. I just wanted to text you to see if you still needed my help and if you looked at your schedule at all.

Locking the screen of my phone, I set it back

down on the desk beside me and turn my attention back to my laptop. I don't expect a response from him immediately, but I can't help but look at my phone from the corner of my eye every few minutes until the screen lights up as a new message comes through.

My heart pounds erratically in my chest and I silently curse it for betraying me in such a way. I shouldn't be excited by the thought of him responding to me. This isn't a friendship; this has no room to grow into something more. It's simply an arrangement between the two of us.

CAMERON

> Hey! I didn't forget about you. I literally just walked in the door from a late practice this evening. I looked at my schedule and have random times during the middle of the day open, or else late evenings. On Tuesdays and Thursdays, we have off-ice weight training and those nights are usually over earlier than actual practice.

I reread his message a few times, before grabbing my calendar to check over what times I have free during the day. Since I don't partake in the normal college activities, my evenings are typically free. Either reserved for my own studying or just binge-reading or watching stuff on Netflix.

ASPEN

> What times are you usually done on Tuesdays and Thursdays? Why don't we make it a point to meet for at least an hour or however long you need on those two evenings? And then we can figure out any times during the day. I have some time between classes on different days, but maybe we can try and coordinate them better.

My message sends and I stare at my phone, a smile touching my lips as the small three bubbles instantly pop up in the bottom corner of the thread. Cam's response comes through almost immediately.

CAMERON

> Want to meet on Thursday and we can figure out some times during the day we can meet? I should be done around seven, if that's not too late for you. I've heard Delilah refer to you as a grandma in class before, so I don't want to be interrupting any of your evening shows or early bedtimes.

My heart hammers in its cage and a stupid smile

is on my lips as I shake my head at my phone. A
wave of shock passes through me as realization hits
me. We may not have talked at all before, but he's
implying that he's noticed me. He's listened to
Delilah and me enough to know my evening habits.

ASPEN

For your information, I am not a
grandma. And let's meet at seven-
thirty in the library?

CAMERON

Sounds good, granny.

Rolling my eyes, I can't stop the chuckle as it
falls from my lips and I reread his stupid message.

ASPEN

You know, you're an ass.

CAMERON

It's all part of my charm, sweets.
Get to know me better and
you'll see.

My stomach flutters and I stare at the screen
with my eyes wide. I don't want his charm because I
refuse to fall under his spell like all these other girls

do. Cameron Sawyer has one thing he cares about and I'm not about to let myself get involved with someone who will never put me first.

Plus, from what I've heard, he doesn't do commitment and I'm not a fling type of girl. I dated the same guy my entire four years of high school and lost my virginity to him. Since being in college, I have yet to hook up with anyone because it seems like they all want the same thing. And I'm not here to be someone's booty call. It's not worth the risk of developing feelings that will never be reciprocated.

What the hell are you even thinking about, Aspen?

Shaking my head at myself, I let out a frustrated sigh as I mentally smack my palm against my forehead. Cam's a smooth talker, a charmer, and he knows it. The last thing that will let happen is letting that affect me.

We agreed to me helping him by tutoring him, so that's exactly what I'm going to do. I'm going to stay true to my word, follow through on it, and then we can go our separate ways. If we become friends, I'm not saying that I would have anything against that, but it can never be anything more.

Cameron might think that he's God's gift to women, but he's got it wrong when it comes to me.

The only thing he is to me is a nuisance right now.

He's persistent as hell, but he doesn't know how much resolve I have. The last thing I'm going to do is develop feelings for him, because I can let his charm roll off me without it having any effect on me.

And Cameron Sawyer is about to realize that I'm not as easy as these other girls he's tried to smooth talk. He can save his sweet nothings for someone else, because I won't be hearing them.

I have goals of my own and I'm not letting the university's biggest playboy mess that up.

CHAPTER FIVE
CAMERON

I haven't spoken to Aspen since the night we set our days to meet for tutoring. That was Monday evening after practice. I could have met with her on Tuesday, but I already had plans with the guys after our off-ice workouts. It would have been too suspicious if I canceled at the last minute, and the last thing I need is any of them digging around for more information.

That's the way it works between all of us. There aren't many secrets kept between us, as we're all practically like brothers. Everyone knows each other's business, except a few things are kept private. Like the fact that Logan was in love with August's little sister. That shit went on for a long time before anyone found out.

Thankfully, it all worked out in the end and they ended up together. If not, I'm not sure what would have happened between August and Logan. That's a line that once you cross it, there's no going back. Things could have gone a lot worse for them, but August came to his senses and realized that Logan was the best thing for Isla.

It was surprising to all of us. Logan kept it under wraps from us all, even though he was acting suspicious and we all had our theories that it involved a girl. None of us knew it was Isla until their little secret finally surfaced.

My secret, however, isn't one I want to come to light. I can't afford to have them afraid that I'm going to let them down. They're my damn family. I refuse to be the one who disappoints them all.

It's been strange seeing Aspen in class and keeping our little secret. It would be unusual for the two of us to be seen talking since we were never really friends. It was almost as if there was a mutual decision made between the two of us without either of us actually discussing it. Nothing changed with the way that we interacted—or lack thereof, should I say.

Sweat drips down the sides of my face as I finish up my workout and my muscles are aching. You would think that it would get easier, but Coach has been pushing us harder each day, knowing regionals are approaching. We all need to be in top shape and performing like we never have.

It was a struggle getting through the evening workout with the anxiety rolling in my stomach. I've never had to have someone tutor me before, so I'm not sure how this is going to work out, but I fucking need it to. This is my last-ditch effort and I'm relying on Aspen to help me get through this.

"Yo, Cam," Hayden calls out my name as we head back to the locker room to shower. "What are you up to tonight? I think Simon and I were going to head to the bar and get some food. We all know that Logan and August are too whipped to tag along all the time."

August narrows his eyes at Hayden as we all head to our lockers. "Did you forget that I have a pregnant girlfriend? Perhaps that might be a little more important than drinking my sorrows away."

"Who said anything about drinking away any sorrows?" Hayden quips as he pulls his shirt over his head. "Sorry that not all of us are tied down already."

"And is there something wrong with that?" Logan questions him as he grabs his things to head to the shower. "It sounds like you might be a little jealous, King."

Hayden chuckles, shaking his head. "Absolutely not. You guys can have fun with your commitments. I'm perfectly fine doing my own thing."

"You'll see how things change when you find the person you can't get out of your head," Logan informs him, leaving the three of us standing there as he disappears into the shower room.

"And that is one thing that will never happen," Hayden replies, glancing at August and I. "Some of us have no interest in ever being tied down to anyone."

August laughs at him, rolling his eyes. "I said the same thing and look at me now."

"Yeah, well, getting someone knocked up isn't exactly on my agenda either," Hayden tells him as he grabs his things and turns back to me as August disappears from where we're standing. "So, what do you say, Cam? I know you don't have anything else going on like the two of them."

"I'm sorry, bro, I can't tonight."

Hayden's eyebrows draw together. "Not you too."

A chuckle slips from my lips and no one notices that it's forced as I shake my head. "Nah, trust me, I don't plan on following in their footsteps. I just have other plans."

"With who?" Simon asks as he strides toward us, freshly showered and dressed. "Come on, man. If you're not with one of us, it's gotta be a girl."

"Oh, fuck off," I tell the two of them as they stare at me expectantly with their cocky smirks and eyebrows raised. "It's nothing like that. I have a shit-load of studying to do and a girl in my class offered me her notes."

"Who is—" Hayden starts, but I quickly shut him down, shaking my head as I walk away.

"Nope, we're not doing this."

I hear Hayden's laughter as I make my way to the showers and slip inside, stripping out of my clothes before stepping into the hot water. I can still hear him and Simon talking shit, but that's what they do. Shit, it's what we all do. But the difference here is, I'm not taking the bait. They don't need to know about this arrangement.

All that they need to know when it comes to Aspen is she's giving me her notes. They don't need to know that she's actually going to be tutoring me too.

————

When I arrive on campus, the parking lot is practically empty. The library usually stays open until ten during the week, since a lot of students need to use the resources in there. I'm not sure what most colleges do, but that's one of the things our university offers and I'm thankful for it at this moment.

With how crazy my schedule is and not being able to get here until seven-thirty, it's a relief knowing that we have enough time to hopefully work through all of this.

As I step through the doors of the library, I notice there are a few students scattered among different tables. Surveying the vast space, I don't see Aspen sitting at any of the tables in my immediate vision. Walking through the room, I round one of the rows of books that leads to another area that has more tables when I see her.

Aspen is tucked away in a corner, her back facing me. Her raven-colored hair is pulled up in a messy bun on the top of her head, and I notice she has a pair of AirPods in as she flips through the pages of her textbook. Her other hand moves as she jots something down on the notebook beside her.

A smile touches my lips as I notice she's wearing a hoodie and a pair of sweats. She had no intention of trying to impress me. In fact, I think she was trying to do the exact opposite. As I round the table, she catches sight of me, lifting her eyes to mine. Her face is free of any makeup and her soft sage irises shine back at me.

I've noticed the light makeup she wears during school hours, but honestly, she doesn't need it. She's naturally beautiful and looks even better with a clean face. A smirk forms on my lips as her tactics aren't fucking working on me. Either she doesn't care about how she looks or she wants to appear unattractive, but it has quite the opposite effect on me.

She's fucking gorgeous.

Aspen pulls her AirPods from her ears and sets them down on the table in front of her. "Hey," she says softly, smiling at me as I pull out the chair across from her and sit down. "Sorry, I was just working on some things for one of my other classes."

"What are you majoring in?" I ask her, the question random as I look over what appears to be some type of math that I sure as hell would never be able to do in my life.

"Pre-med," she tells me, a bashful smile on her lips as she bats her eyelashes. "What about you?"

"Marketing," I answer her with a shrug. "Not exactly something that interests me, but it's something to fall back on if hockey doesn't work out."

Her eyebrows draw together, a playful look in her eyes. "Is Cameron Sawyer really doubting his abilities to play professional hockey? Where's the Cam that I'm actually supposed to be tutoring right now?"

A soft laugh falls from my lips and I roll my eyes at her. "You know what I mean. It's always safe to have a fallback plan. You never know what is going to happen. I could easily get injured and poof—there goes everything I've worked for."

She stares at me for a moment, her smile falling. "Okay, enough of the pessimism. If there's one thing you need to know about me, positive energy is the only thing that is acceptable."

"You weren't exactly exuding positive energy when I first asked you for your help," I quip, a smirk on my lips.

Aspen's expression softens and she offers me an apologetic smile. "Sorry about that. It just seemed kind of weird and caught me off guard. I didn't mean to be abrasive and appear cold. I have some trust issues occasionally, especially with people that I don't know."

"Well, it's a good thing we're going to be spending so much time together," I retort, winking at her. "That way you'll be able to get to know me a little better."

"Who said I want to get to know you?" she throws back at me, a ghost of a smile playing on her lips as mischief sparkles in her soft sage irises.

I shrug, a look of indifference passing over my face. "We'll see what happens."

"How about we see how terribly you're doing in bio so we can figure out how much work is going to be needed to get you back on track?"

Her question thrusts me back into reality, away from the flirtatious behavior between the two of us. Swallowing hard, I nod. "Good idea."

Aspen stares at me for a moment, her expression unreadable before she closes her math book and slides it to the other side of her. Grabbing her biology book and notes, she flips to where we are in our studies right now.

"What are you struggling with the most?" she asks me, no judgment in her voice, only curiosity. "I need some type of a baseline for us to start."

A nervous chuckle escapes me. "Um... everything?"

"Why are you even taking a biology course if you're majoring in marketing?"

Her question catches me off guard for a moment. "Honestly, I don't know. It was listed as a class I needed my freshman year and I literally pushed it off until now because I knew it wasn't something I was ever good at. I barely passed the class in high school and I was going to try to get out of taking it, but it was too late."

"Okay. So, do you understand the basic stuff that we've gone over in class? Or do you need me to start from square one? Because if we have to do that, it might take a long time."

"Fuck no," I tell her, shaking my head rapidly. "I just need to literally bring my grade up to a C. So, if we can just focus on the stuff we're learning now and I can pass the tests coming up, then I'm good to go."

Aspen nods. "Well, let's get to it then."

We spend the next two hours with me staring at her, attempting to retain everything she's explaining to me. It's confusing as fuck, but she breaks it down, taking her time to explain everything to me in a way I am able to understand.

By the time we finish, I feel like I have a better understanding of the material, although I am nowhere close to being able to pass a test with the score I need to raise my overall grade. Aspen finishes up, her pale, sage eyes searching mine.

"I hope some of this made sense to you," she offers softly as she closes her books and slides them into her bag. "I know it's a lot to try and remember, but we can try different things to help you get there."

"No, everything you did so far was perfect," I tell her with honesty, momentarily getting lost in the green depths of her irises. "It makes a hell of a lot more sense than it did listening to our professor drone on. I think these one-on-one sessions are exactly what I need."

Watching her throat bob as she swallows hard, I don't miss the way a pink tint creeps across her cheeks. I bite back the smirk that plays on my lips, reveling in the notion that I have some type of an effect on her.

Get it together, Sawyer. She's here to tutor you, not fall into your lap and into your bed.

"What does your daily schedule look like during the week?" I ask her as we both rise from our seats and begin to walk through the library. "I have, like, an hour-and-a-half break between classes around noon on Mondays, Wednesdays, and Fridays."

She pauses for a second, chewing on the inside of her cheek before she nods. "That could work for me. I have a break around the same time, too, and usually end up in here."

"Not only are you a grandma, but you're quite the bookworm too, huh?"

Aspen rolls her eyes at me, shoving her shoulder into mine. "Hey. Some of us aren't star athletes and actually have to worry about a career that doesn't involve playing a sport after we graduate. And, I need to be on top of my grades if I want to get into med school after this."

Pulling open the door, I hold it for her as she walks through, quietly thanking me. "You know, you're pretty inspiring, Aspen Rossi."

She glances over at me, a sad smile touching her lips. "I learned from a young age not to depend on someone else. I want to make a life for myself—create a safety net—that way I don't have to worry about relying on anyone else."

My eyebrows draw together, so many questions on the tip of my tongue, but I clamp my mouth shut and swallow them back. It's none of my business and if Aspen wants to share, I'll wait for her to feel comfortable enough to tell me.

If there's one thing I've found out about Aspen

Rossi in the past two hours I've spent with her, it is that she isn't who she appears to be to the rest of the world.

There's more to her than she lets on.

And I fully intend on peeling back her layers and figuring out who the fuck she really is.

CHAPTER SIX
ASPEN

"Girl, please come out with me tonight," Delilah begs as she flops down onto the couch in my living room area. "I know that you hate going to parties, but it's my birthday this weekend and it would mean the world to me if you came out. Even if it's just this one time."

Sitting down on the loveseat opposite of her, I pull my legs up and tuck my feet underneath me. "You really know how to lay on the guilt, don't you?"

Delilah bats her fake eyelashes at me, smiling sweetly as she gives me puppy dog eyes. "I wouldn't call it guilt. I just know how to be persuasive. And let's be real, when was the last time you went to a party?"

"Um, I think I went with you to one at the beginning of the year and it was a goddamn shit show."

"Oh yeah," Delilah mumbles, scrunching her face up. "Derek got really trashed and tried to kiss you, didn't he?"

My eyes widen and my nostrils flare. "Oh no, he successfully kissed me without my permission and was a dick when I turned him down. Remember how much shit he talked?"

Delilah nods, giving me a sympathetic smile. "Yeah, I'm sorry about that. I mean, I kind of thought he had a thing for you, but I didn't see that coming at all."

"Don't forget about the fact that you got blackout drunk and puked in my car too."

Delilah winces, a frown forming on her face before she breaks out into a string of laughter. "Okay, yeah, that night was a complete shit show. But, you were, like, the best at taking care of me, so I'm forever grateful to you for that."

Thankfully, I don't really drink. I had a nice buzz that night off of two drinks, but I could still function. I was possibly the only person at that party who was coherent enough to act like a normal human being. Things were going well until Derek tried to make his move, and then Delilah getting sick was just the icing on the cake.

I knew it wasn't my scene before that night, but the chain of events confirmed that I was not cut out for college parties at all. There was a part of me that wanted to let loose, just one time while I'm here, but at the same time, I don't really want to get to the point that some of these kids get to.

"So, will you please come?" Delilah tries again, rolling onto her side on the couch as she props her head on her hand. "I promise I will behave and Derek knows to stay away from you after that night."

Staring back at her, she gives me a look of desperation, and I sigh in defeat. This is part of my problem—I have such a hard time telling people no for the fear of disappointing them. "Fine, I will go."

"Shut up!" Delilah quickly sits up, a smile consuming her lips as she claps her hands together. "You're really going to come with me? I promise you won't have to babysit me this time."

"Yes, I will come. And no, you aren't dressing me. I'm going to wear what I want and do what I want while I'm there, okay?" I warn her, narrowing my eyes. "Our college experiences don't have to be the same, but since it's your birthday and you're practically leaving me no choice, I'll go."

Delilah quickly jumps to her feet. "You're the best, Aspen," she beams at me as she digs her keys from her purse. "I'm going to head back to my dorm and get ready. Did you want to meet me on campus and we can walk there since it's only, like, two blocks away?"

"Sure, that works," I tell her, smiling back as she practically skips to the door. As much as I don't want to go, there's a part of me that is a little excited. The thought of going out makes me a little anxious, but maybe my best friend is right. Maybe I do need to broaden my horizons in terms of my college experience.

After all... life is too short.

And like Cam said, you never know when something is going to happen that could take it all away from you.

―――――

Settling for a light gray oversized sweater, I pair it with some black leggings and a pair of black Vans. It's still cold in Vermont at this time of the year, so I make sure to grab my winter coat and shrug it on. I only applied my normal amount of makeup, since I'm not going to the party to impress anyone. If anything, it's just to make myself feel a little more human.

Grabbing a beanie, I pull it down over the top of my head. I've been blessed with long black hair that has its own natural waves. It's nice because it's low maintenance so it doesn't require me to regularly style my hair. On special occasions, I might straighten it or throw in some curls, but this isn't a special occasion.

It's a college party where everyone's going to end up getting trashed, except for me. There are a few rare exceptions at these parties, but most of those people just smoke weed instead of drink, so we still end up on different levels. I don't plan on getting drunk, but a drink or two is definitely in my future.

Pulling onto campus, I find a parking spot near the dorms and send Delilah a text, letting her know that I'm here. As I walk through the cold toward her building, she meets me on the sidewalk out front. Delilah isn't dressed for the weather and is definitely in her full-on party attire. She looks like she should be going to a party in the summer, with a short bodycon dress hugging her curves.

Her long legs are bare and her heels add a few inches to her height, which has her standing almost a full head taller than me. Delilah put on her night-time makeup with a heavy smoky eye and she has contoured the fuck out of her face to create the illusion that her cheekbones are higher than they actually are.

Don't get me wrong, she's a goddamn bombshell and I would never judge her for the way she dresses or the makeup she wears. It just shows the stark contrast between the two of us. You wouldn't think so if you saw us during the daytime, since we're practically two peas in a pod. But when it comes time to party, we couldn't be more opposite.

Delilah pulls me in for a hug and we begin our walk toward the party. She goes on about how she hopes that Alexander is here tonight. We both have a class with him and Delilah has been talking to him for a little bit, but nothing has happened between the two of them. She's had her sights set on him for a while and I know she wants to take their friendship to the next level.

It's hard to miss the house as we walk up to it. It's already crowded outside, with a group of people on the front porch along with another in the front yard. They're all drinking, like it doesn't matter if the cops show up and find everyone is underage. Shaking my head, I follow Delilah in through the front door. It's completely packed inside, with the lights dim and the loud bass of the speakers pounding through the house.

I have to hand it to some of the students here. They really know how to throw a banger, even if it isn't my scene. Delilah grabs my hand, leading me through the sea of people dancing and drinking until we reach the kitchen. In the center of the room, there's a keg and she grabs two plastic cups, filling them both with the frothy beer before handing one to me.

My lip curls up in disgust as I look at the dark yellow liquid sloshing around in the cup. "You know, I really kind of hate beer."

Delilah laughs, rolling her eyes at me. "Yeah, I know. You hate anything that could be remotely fun. I'll be honest, though, it does taste pretty disgusting, but it gets better the more you drink it."

"I said I would drink, I didn't say I was going to get trashed like you do."

Delilah shrugs. "Whatever. You letting loose a little bit is still a win in my book. Now, come play beer pong with me if we can get on the table."

She wraps her hand around mine and I take a

sip, needing the liquid courage as she drags me through the house. We end up in a random room that has two tables set up, each one already in the full swing of games as people toss ping pong balls into the cups. I've played a few times and tend to get a little competitive, even without drinking.

Delilah tells the one guy that we're playing next and he reluctantly agrees, although I'm sure there's already a list of people waiting their turn. Delilah has an uncanny way of getting her way through various forms of manipulation. Lifting my beer to my lips, I take another sip of the liquid, regretting it as I taste the bitter flavor on my tongue.

"Drink up," she shouts over the loud music that plays in the background. "I'm going to go get us two more cups, because you know we have to drink during the game."

"Do I really have to?" I groan, my shoulders sagging. I hate the taste of this shit and really don't want to drink any more. "I've played before without drinking."

Delilah rolls her eyes. "Suit yourself," she says, waving her hand as she spins on her heel. "I'll be right back."

Standing off to the side of the table, my eyes scan the room, noticing different students that I've seen on campus or in class. A loud laugh sounds from the doorway on the opposite side and my stomach drops as I see Cameron and Asher, another hockey player, come strolling into the room. Two other guys from their team trail behind them.

Cam pauses, his gaze meeting mine, and he raises an eyebrow in curiosity. Tilting my head to the side, I offer him a nervous smile, shifting my weight on my feet. He stops for a moment, assessing me from across the room as I lift my beer and take a long swig. I didn't feel the need to drink until this moment.

But I have a feeling I might need more alcohol than this to get me through this party.

CHAPTER SEVEN
CAMERON

Well, isn't this quite the surprise.

This is the first time that I've seen Aspen at a party, no less with a beer in her hand. She never struck me as the type who liked to drink and considering the fact that I've never seen her out before, I figured this wasn't really her scene. And to be honest, she looks a little out of place. Like she's stepped out of her comfort zone for the first time and isn't sure what she's supposed to do.

Lifting my cup, I cheers her through the air and drain the rest of my beer as she takes a small sip of hers.

"Who's that?" Simon questions me, his voice low after having just watched our silent interaction. "I've seen her around campus, I think."

I nod, watching as her friend, Delilah, joins her and hands her another plastic cup. "Aspen. I have a few classes with her. She's pretty quiet and keeps to herself, but we've been talking a little."

Asher cocks an eyebrow. "Oh shit. A new prospect for you? What happened to the last girl?"

"Julia?" I ask him, shaking my head as a soft laugh falls from my lips. "You know how it goes. Just a distraction and nothing more. We ended shit because she wanted more and not with me... not that I wanted more anyways."

Simon shrugs. "Hey, we all do it, there's no judgment or shame."

"Except for Logan and August," Hayden cuts in as a chuckle vibrates from his chest. "Those two are so pussy-whipped. I have no plans of ever falling into that same trap."

"Yeah, I'm good with the way things are," I agree with him, tapping my cup to his as we both drink. "You wanna try and get on the table?"

"Hell yeah," Hayden grins. "Let me go get another beer and I'll check how many people are already on the list. You want another one?"

Draining my cup, I nod and hand it to him. "I'll see about getting on the table. Get me two cups."

Hayden disappears and I watch Asher, Simon,

and Sterling disappear through the doorway into the other room where everyone's dancing. I don't know what they're all planning on doing, but I know they're trying to get laid tonight, so to each their own.

Just as I'm about to walk over to John, who's controlling who is on the tables, the game on the nearest table ends. Glancing over, I see Delilah and Aspen making their way to the end of it and begin setting the cups back up. Aspen grabs the pitcher of water and fills them back up to their respective depth.

Two other guys are setting up the cups on the other end, but this is my perfect opportunity. I stride over to John. "Put King and I on the table now," I demand, my hard gaze meeting his.

John swallows hard and shakes his head in defeat. "Sorry, man, you know how it goes. You gotta get on the list and when it's your turn, then you can play. Unless Anderson and Cash want to switch with you."

Spinning on my heel, I turn my back to John and march over to Anderson and Cash. They both lift their heads, their eyebrows both drawing together as I stop in front of them.

"Yo, I have a huge favor to ask both of you," I say,

dropping my voice just above a whisper as I lean down near them. "I need you guys to switch with King and I."

"Bro, do you know how long we've been waiting for our turn?" Anderson cuts his tone at me. Cash elbows him, giving him a knowing look as Hayden walks up beside me.

Hayden glances over at me. "What's going on? You get us on the list?"

I don't take my eyes away from Anderson and Cash. "Yeah, I'm just trying to get these two to switch with us."

"Hm," Hayden muses, a smirk forming on his lips as he sees Aspen and Delilah at the other end of the table. "You two are cool, right?" Hayden questions them. "I don't really know either of you, but I would imagine that you don't want to run into any trouble or anything."

Cash shakes his head. "You guys can totally take our turn."

"What the hell are you doing?" Anderson barks at him. "There's a list for a reason. Just because you guys run the fucking hockey team doesn't mean you get to call the shots everywhere you go."

"Are you forgetting that the hockey team is essentially what makes this school what it is?"

Hayden questions him, tilting his head to the side as his gaze grows colder. "Don't forget, we're going to be here another year after this one. We can make your life a living hell if we want to."

My stomach churns because violence isn't where I was headed with this. Actually, I don't know where the hell King is really going with all of this, but this is how he rolls. He's not afraid of making threats, even if they end up being empty. Hayden King is used to getting what he wants and he isn't going to take no for an answer from these two assholes.

"Fine," Anderson caves, and Cash sighs in relief. "We'll switch with you guys this one time, but that's it. Never again, you got it? I'm not fucking afraid of you guys."

Hayden leans closer to him, plucking the ping pong ball from his grip. "Perhaps you should be."

Anderson scoffs, cutting his eyes at Hayden before Cash grabs his arm and they step away. Hayden steps up to the table, grabbing the other ball before handing it to me. As I take it from him, my lips are pursed with a scolding look on my face.

"What?" He shrugs, feigning innocence. "Your girl is playing and you wanted to play against her, right? I was just making sure that it happened."

"You can't go around threatening everyone every

time you don't get your way," I remind him, dipping my ball down into the cup before I tap my finger against it, shaking off the excess water. "People are different here. We might be the top of the food chain with being on the roster, but you can't manipulate everyone into getting what you want."

"And why the hell not? If I have some type of power, I'm going to use it to my advantage," he admits with no shame whatsoever in his voice. This is how Hayden has always been. He knows how to work people, how to fuck the system. And he isn't afraid to do whatever he has to. He has yet to meet someone who actually challenged him back. "I never threatened any type of bodily harm or said that I would follow through on any of them. I simply just let them know that the next two years could be easy or hard for them."

"All because of a game of beer pong?"

Hayden narrows his eyes at me. "Did you want to play Aspen or not? Jesus fuck."

"Are the two of you going to argue all night long or can we get started?" Delilah's singsong voice interrupts our dispute, grabbing our attention. We both turn to look at them, only my eyes find Aspen's instead of Delilah's.

Aspen is staring at me with a slightly confused

look in her eyes, but there's a challenge behind her facade. She knows we weren't supposed to be playing them and I can see the questions floating around in that beautiful mind of hers. Too bad she isn't going to have the opportunity to ask any of them.

"Let's go," Hayden tells the two of them as he and Delilah set up for who gets to shoot first. Delilah misses her shot as Hayden sinks his ball in the very first cup. There's a displeased look on her face and she rolls her eyes as Hayden high-fives me.

We both take our shots, Hayden making the same cup as before and mine just bouncing off the lip of one in the back row. I'm usually better than this and we can clear the table before the other team even gets a shot in. Right now, though, under Aspen's gaze, I can't help but feel like I'm not on top of my game.

The need to impress her is there, but I'm competitive as hell.

She wants to play, but she needs to understand that I only play to win.

Delilah and Aspen both take sips of their beers before taking their turns. Delilah misses hers and lets out an exaggerated groan. I watch Aspen as she steps closer to the table, her gaze focused on the cups as she lines up her shot. She pulls her arm back before thrusting it forward and releases the ball, her shot completely effortless as it drops into one of the cups.

"Damn," Hayden smirks, shaking his head as the two of us take a drink. "You bring a ringer with you tonight, Delilah?"

She lifts her middle finger to him. "Fuck off, King," she laughs. "You have no idea what's about to hit you with Aspen finally playing."

"Hey, I play sometimes."

"I think it was just a lucky shot," I interject, my gaze trained on Aspen's. "We run the table, so I'd like to see the two of you actually try and take us down."

"Oh yeah?" Aspen challenges me, raising an eyebrow. "Let's see what you got, pretty boy."

My heart hammers in my chest, a smirk forming on my lips at the slip of her words. The alcohol must be loosening her up, because this isn't the uptight Aspen I'm used to. She's usually quiet and soft-spoken, but here she is challenging me with an arrogance that has my cock throbbing.

Challenge fucking accepted.

CHAPTER EIGHT
ASPEN

Delilah's gaze is on the side of my face and when I turn to look at her, she raises an eyebrow. I shouldn't have agreed to drink because regret instantly floods me as soon as I realize that I called Cam pretty boy. This is exactly why I don't drink. Once I start getting a buzz, it's like I lose control of all of my inhibitions. Thankfully, my meds have already worn off from earlier in the day, because that is a combination I don't enjoy at all.

But I must admit, the warmth spreading through my body feels pretty nice right now. I feel like I can finally breathe without a weight on my chest. Tearing my eyes away from hers, I meet Cam's gaze across the table, his lips lifted in a grin as he stares me down.

Hayden makes his shot and it effortlessly lands in a cup. Cam doesn't take his eyes away from mine, following suit as he makes it in too. Delilah throws her hands up in an uproar as I grab both of the balls and roll them across the table to them. Grabbing the cups, I slide them out of the way.

"There's no way that the two of you are making those shots again," I tell them, attempting to talk shit and get into their heads. It's worked in the past, as a tactic to shake up an opponent and throw them off their game. With the way Hayden and Cameron are smirking at me, I don't think it's something that will work on either of them.

Delilah and I both grab our cups of beer, taking long swigs as the boys toss their balls across the table. Neither one makes it in and for that, I am eternally grateful. I may not have gotten into their heads, but they still didn't make the shots, so it makes me feel a little better about talking shit.

We go back and forth, throwing ping pong balls at cups filled with water, all of us talking shit to each other as we drain our drinks. The game goes on for longer than anyone expects, until we're down to only one cup each. Delilah was right, the beer does go down better the more you drink. And I'm well on my way to being drunker than I've been since high school.

A crowd has since grown around the table, everyone watching in awe and cheering us on as we continue to shoot our shots. I don't know if it's because everyone has gotten pretty drunk at this point, but all four of us are shooting air balls. Even though we haven't been hitting any cups, we all continued to drink, which has led us to this inevitable moment.

Delilah fumbles with her ball and it slips from her hands, rolling off the table and onto the floor on my side. Abandoning my spot at the table, I start walking to get it at the same time that Cameron starts to move. We both bend down at the same time, just nearly bumping our heads as our hands touch around the ball. I wrap my fingers around the sphere as Cam encapsulates my hand with his own.

We're both crouched down, his hand covering mine as his deep green eyes search mine. A heat creeps up my neck, spreading across my cheeks as his gaze drops down to my lips. I can't tear my eyes away from him, watching as his tongue darts out and he wets his lips before looking back up at me.

"Damn, Aspen," Cam mumbles, shaking his

head at me as a ghost of a smile plays on his lips. "Can't you just lose already?"

"Absolutely not," I retort, straightening my spine as I push my shoulders back. "Believe it or not, I'm actually pretty competitive and this game just so happens to be something that I'm actually good at."

Cam tilts his head to the side, his eyebrows pulling together slightly. "There's a lot of things you're good at. Not just beer pong."

A soft laugh falls from my lips as I study his face for a moment, his features appearing to be tormented as he looks at me thoughtfully. "Let's be real... the only thing I'm actually good at is related to studying and school shit. I'm not athletic, I'm not artistic. I'm just your average nerd."

Cameron's lips curl upward, a fire burning in the depths of his eyes as he stares back at me. "You're the best nerd I know. Dare I say, my favorite?"

"I find it hard to believe that you're friends with any other nerds," I snort, rolling my eyes as the alcohol allows me to let my guard down. My calves begin to ache from the way we're still crouched down and I rise back up. Cam follows along with me, slowly removing his hand from mine. As soon as it's gone, I miss his warmth and resist the urge to demand he put it back.

"So, we're friends now?" he questions me, the flames licking at me as I tiptoe closer to the fire that burns in him.

I shrug, my body swaying slightly from the alcohol. Dropping my hands to the table, I brace myself, feeling Cameron's arm sliding around my back as he grips me around the waist. "I'm fine," I mumble, glancing over at Delilah, who is too busy with Alexander. "Ugh."

"Let's go outside and get some fresh air and maybe some water."

Nodding, I look back to Cam and throw my arm around his shoulders as he walks with me, still holding on to my waist. I'm fairly certain that I could walk by myself, but I'm pretty drunk and he smells good. Too good that I don't want him to move away from me right now. I like him this close, even if it's the last thing I'll admit when I'm sober.

A drunken mind speaks sober thoughts.

Cam leads me outside, grabbing two waters as we pass through the kitchen. There are a few people out on the back patio, but he finds a bench that isn't occupied by anyone and sets me down. He follows along, sitting down beside me as he unscrews the top of the water bottle and hands it to me.

Lifting the rim to my lips, I tilt it back and

swallow some of the cold liquid. Looking back at
Cam, I find his gaze on mine, studying me as he
watches me put the lid back on my bottle of water.

"Since we're friends, can I tell you something?"

Swallowing hard over my buzz, I nod. I don't
trust my voice in this moment with the way that
Cameron is looking at me. Both of our heads are
turned toward each other, the only thing touching is
our thighs pressed together. Cam's eyes are filled
with a burning desire as they slowly move back and
forth between mine.

"You're fucking breathtaking."

A heat creeps up my neck, spreading across my
cheeks as the warmth spreads through my body. My
eyes widen as I stare back at him, completely taken
aback by his admission. I choke out a laugh, the
sound getting caught in my throat.

"You're only saying that because you're drunk," I
respond, my voice soft as I recover from my embar-
rassing choking episode.

Cam reaches toward me, lightly brushing a piece
of hair from my face before tucking it behind my ear.
"Can I tell you another secret?" he asks me, leaning
closer.

My breath catches in my throat and I nod as he
leans even closer, his lips brushing against the outer

shell of my ear. He's overwhelming my senses as I inhale the smell of his cologne. He smells like a mix of the forest and bourbon.

"I'm not drunk."

Swallowing hard, my heart pounds erratically in my chest as his fingertips trail down my neck and he rests his palm against my collarbone. He doesn't pull away at first, his breath still warm against my skin as his lips lightly brush my ear again.

"Aspen," he breathes, the sultry sound of his voice wrapping itself around my eardrums. A shiver creeps up my spine, feeling the warmth of his hand through my sweater.

Holding my breath, I wait for him to say something else but he doesn't. He lifts his hand away from my collarbone and moves back, his breath leaving the side of my neck. My eyes desperately search his and my body sways from the alcohol as a ragged breath slips from my lips.

There's a look of torment lingering in his stormy eyes as he stares directly through me. "How are you getting home?" he questions me, his voice strained.

Shrugging, I chew on the inside of my cheek. "I met Delilah at campus and we walked here. I don't even know where she is now, though..."

"I'm pretty sure I saw her disappear somewhere

with Alexander." Cameron pauses for a moment, his eyes searching mine. "I'll walk back with you and drive you home, because there's no way in hell I'm letting you get behind the wheel right now."

"I'll be fine," I tell him, brushing away the feelings as his rejection lingers in the air. He didn't flat-out reject me, but he got close and then backed off, the tension around us building. If he actually wanted me, he would have acted on it instead of pulling away. "I'm sure I'll be sober enough to drive by the time I get back to my car."

"Nope," he says, popping up to his feet. He pulls out his phone and taps on the screen before holding it up to his ear. "Yo, Hayden. I'm gonna drive Aspen's car back to her apartment. I need you to pick me up there."

I watch him and he's silent for a moment, listening to Hayden speak to him before he ends the call and slips it back into the pocket of his jeans. He extends his arm, offering his hand to me. Dropping my gaze to it, I stare at it for a moment, unsure of what the right move is to make. I'm just supposed to be tutoring him. I don't have to be his friend, and I sure as hell don't need to get close to him.

A sigh slips from my lips and his palm feels warm against mine as I place my hand in his. He lifts me to my feet, making sure I'm steady before he leads me around the side of the house. We bypass everyone still partying hard and I make a mental note to text Delilah and let her know that I went home.

We step onto the sidewalk and Cam falls into step beside me, his hand still in mine as we walk through the brisk night back toward campus. My body sways slightly, but I don't stumble as the cool air helps with the buzz I had going.

"I'm sorry if I was misleading," Cam says quietly as we approach the parking lot to the campus. He follows along with me as I walk closer to my car and he moves with me over to the passenger's side. As I pull out my keys, he takes them from me and unlocks the door before pulling it open for me.

As I drop down into the seat, my eyes meet his. I get lost for a moment, watching the storm clouds roll in his pupils before he closes the door and walks over to the driver's side. He slides in behind the wheel, pulling the door closed, and starts the engine.

We fall into an uncomfortable silence, the tension hanging heavily in the air as he pulls the car out of the parking lot. I stare at him and he glances over as he stops the car at the stop sign. "Where do you live? I need directions to your place."

I tell him my address and the apartment complex I live in and he seems to already know where it is. He pulls out his phone, I'm assuming to text Hayden, before he begins to drive without needing any further direction.

The silence is deafening and the alcohol still coursing through my system gives me a boost of courage I don't necessarily want.

"How were you misleading?" I blurt out.

Cam glances over at me before looking back at the road. "I don't want to blur the lines because I can't give you any more than this strange friendship. And I actually need your help and for you to tutor me. I shouldn't have said what I did."

You're fucking breathtaking.

His words float into my head and I feel the sting from him wanting to take back what he said. My stomach sinks and my hand grips the handle on the door as I direct my gaze out the window.

"That doesn't mean I didn't mean it, though," he adds, his voice soft and barely audible.

I don't tear my eyes away from the window, feeling a spark of hope as we pull into the parking lot of my apartment complex. Another car pulls in not long after we park and Cameron and I both get out, him handing me my keys after locking the door.

"Can I walk you to your door?"

Shaking my head, I wrap my arms around my body to shield myself from the cold air of the night. "I'm good, but thank you for driving my car for me. I'll see you in class on Monday."

Cam's jaw tics, but he doesn't say a word as he gives me a curt nod. He lingers, but I don't entertain him any further. Spinning on my heel, I head into the apartment building and press the button for the elevator. As the doors slide open, I chance one last look into the parking lot and see Cameron still standing there, watching me.

A sigh slips from my lips as I step onto the elevator and press the button for my floor.

We have an arrangement for me to tutor him and help him get through the rest of the year. Nothing more than that. Once he gets his grades up, he won't need me anymore. Our so-called friendship was just drunken words spoken into the void.

We're not really friends and I don't think we ever will be.

CHAPTER NINE
CAMERON

Walking into class, I'm not surprised when I see Aspen already sitting in her usual seat toward the front of the class. Delilah is sitting beside her with her head on the table like she's taking a quick nap before the lecture starts. I'm the last one walking in and the seat to the left of Aspen is still open.

She doesn't lift her eyes from her notebook in front of her as I walk in front of the table and drop down into the chair beside her. Staring at the side of her face, I watch her as she struggles to glance in my direction. The point of her pen digs deeper into her paper as she writes something down. I don't know what the hell she could possibly be doing because class hasn't even started, but that's Aspen for you.

Probably organizing her goddamn thoughts on paper like she pre-studied the lecture or some shit.

I can't fault her for how studious she is. If anything, it's admirable and I wish I had half the drive she does. There was a point where I did, and I still do care about my studies, but only to a point. And that point is only to make sure I have passing grades. The only thing that really matters is hockey and that's the only real reason why I'm here.

"Hey," I murmur, my voice loud enough for her to hear me. She glances at me from the corner of her eye, nodding slightly, but she doesn't offer me any words in response.

Leaning closer to her, I inhale her soft floral scent as I peer over her shoulder to see what she's doing. My eyebrows tug together when I see that she isn't doing anything constructive. Instead, it's just mindless doodling, as if she's trying to distract herself from something.

A sigh slips from my lips and I sit back in my seat, pulling my book out onto the table as the professor enters the room and begins to write something across the board. Aspen pays me no mind and it's a fucking struggle trying to focus for the entirety of class.

Every once in a while, Aspen and Delilah speak

to each other in hushed voices but I'm not able to make out any of their words. I just want her to turn in my direction and talk to me, but she doesn't. I know Saturday night didn't go exactly as planned. I wanted to kiss her, but I stopped myself from doing it.

That's one line I can't cross with Aspen. Regardless of how my body reacts to her and how badly I want her. She's something else, but she's something special. And she deserves so much more than I could ever give her. I don't have the time to dedicate myself to someone else right now and as much as I would love to use her as a distraction, that's literally all that it would be.

I can't afford to let someone in. Look at how messy Logan's life got. I mean, this is a little different. I'm not sleeping with my best friend's little sister. But I feel like I hardly see him anymore. That's not to say that being in a relationship is a bad thing, it's just not for everyone and it's definitely not for me.

I've grown comfortable in the way I live my life and I don't need someone disrupting any of that. As much as I'd love to fuck around with Aspen, I need her for more than that. She's my only hope of keeping my scholarship and being able to play in regionals. I need her to help me get through my schooling so I can keep playing.

I've come too far to lose it all now. I mean, shit... I don't even know what I would do without hockey.

Plus, Aspen has her own aspirations to succeed in life. She's here studying pre-med and will be going to graduate school after she finishes next year. There's no room for me in her life, just like there's no room for her in mine.

Although, I'm a little confused after the other night. I thought we had come to terms with being friends, but with the cold shoulder she's giving me right now, I'm not sure she actually meant it.

I wanted to walk her to her apartment, even though I knew it was a bad idea. Part of me was glad when she declined, but I'm also afraid that maybe I offended her in some way. I meant it when I told her that she is breathtaking because, holy fuck, she is. She's an enigma. Maybe she doesn't believe that I actually meant it because of what I said in the car.

It was a misleading comment and I need to rectify this situation without crossing any more lines.

———

Aspen slipped out of class before I had a chance to talk to her. And as much as I wanted to chase her down, I decided to give her some space. It seems like that's what she wants and since we're already supposed to meet during lunch in the library, I'll let her breathe until then.

I barely pay attention in my other classes, but thankfully I have decent grades in them so I don't need to worry. My main issue is biology and as I head to the library, that's the furthest thing from my mind. Instead, it's Aspen that creeps into the darkest corners of my mind, fucking haunting me.

As I walk into the library, she's already sitting at a table waiting for me. All of her notes and books are spread out and she sits there, reading a novel as she waits. Her head lifts, her gaze meeting mine as I stride closer to her. Stopping opposite of her, I reach for the chair, but recoil my hand as I walk around to sit beside her instead.

Aspen inhales sharply, shifting to the side as if she wants to put as much distance between us as possible. She turns in her seat, facing me completely as I sit down and turn my head to look at her. A smile tugs at the corners of my lips as I watch a pink tint spread across her cheeks.

"So, are you still giving me the silent treatment or can we actually talk now?"

Aspen narrows her eyes at me, her eyebrows pulling together. "If we're talking about biology, then sure."

Shaking my head, I fold my arms on the table and stare her down. "Not until we talk about the other night."

"There's nothing to talk about," she says quietly, the harshness lingering in her words. "Nothing happened and I was drunk anyway. I'd honestly prefer to just forget about it and move on, if that's okay with you."

"No, it's not," I retort, watching her recoil in disapproval. "I think you took what I said to you the wrong way."

"Nope," she disagrees, shaking her head as she rolls her eyes. "You made yourself pretty clear. And trust me, I don't want anything more than whatever this is."

My eyebrows draw together as I tilt my head to the side. "So, you were just drunk when you said we were friends, huh?"

She stares at me for a moment. "If I remember correctly, I never said that we were actually friends."

"So, you were the one with the misleading comment then."

"No," she argues, her lips curling upward as she shakes her head at me. "We can be friends, Cameron, as long as we both agree to nothing more than that."

A smile tugs at the corners of my lips.

"You've got yourself a deal, Aspen Rossi."

CHAPTER TEN
ASPEN

"So, are you going to tell me what the hell that was last weekend?" Delilah asks me as she settles into my couch with a carton of ice cream. She's wearing a pair of sweatpants and an oversized hoodie, since it's a cold and rainy day. For a Friday night, this is about as exciting as it is going to get for us.

Delilah is the opposite of me, liking to be more of the center of attention where I just like to fade into the background and go unnoticed. She goes through these periods of being super extroverted and then hiding herself away in my apartment when she doesn't feel like dealing with the rest of the world. I always welcome her company, because, believe it or not, sometimes my life can be lonely.

"I don't know what you're talking about," I tell her, shrugging my shoulders as I turn on the TV and start flipping through the movies on the screen. "Are you going to tell me what happened with Alexander?"

Delilah glances over at me and I can feel her eyes on the side of my head. "Who said anything happened?"

Tearing my gaze from the TV, I look over at her, my lips pursed as I give her a knowing look. "Let's be real, Del. You're hiding away in my apartment with an entire carton of ice cream—not that I'm judging. We just both know that this is what you do when you're avoiding shit and I have a feeling it might have something to do with Alexander."

Her nostrils flare as she sighs, her shoulders hanging heavily in defeat. "I'll tell you if you tell me what the hell is going on between you and Cameron fucking Sawyer."

My heart pounds erratically in my chest at the mere mention of him. Even though we've been meeting throughout the week for our scheduled tutoring sessions, he still has me shaken up. None of that matters, though, because it literally cannot mean a thing.

And who am I kidding? It's definitely just

hormones that have me wishing that our situation was different than it is. It's been a while since I've gotten laid or even bothered to show any interest in pursuing someone else. Perhaps it's just the boredom of my mundane life. I need some excitement and I cannot go looking for that with Cameron fucking Sawyer.

"I slept with Alexander," Delilah admits, her voice quiet as she directs her gaze back to the TV.

My eyebrows tug together as I watch her for a moment while she shoves a spoonful of chocolate ice cream into her mouth. "Isn't that what you wanted?"

Delilah sighs, tilting her head as she looks back at me. "It was terrible. Like, so bad, oh my god, I'm embarrassed for him." She pauses for a moment, dropping her spoon into the carton of ice cream. "Needless to say, it ruined everything because he is, like, in love now and I can't bring myself to break his heart. I like him as a person and his personality is awesome, but the sex... I just can't do it, Aspen."

A chuckle falls from my lips and I shake my head at her, partially in disbelief of the entire situation. "You know, this would be your luck. You've wanted him so badly, to go beyond being friends, and this is the shit that happens."

"I see why you stay single now." She sighs again, pursing her lips. "It's not worth the bullshit. You're almost better if you act like a dude and fuck without attachments. Just hit it and quit it and keep on moving."

I shrug, a smirk creeping onto my face. "Okay, that's totally not me. I haven't slept with anyone since, like, summer. But yeah... being single is definitely better. Or at least keeping everything free from any types of feelings."

Cameron lingers in the back of my mind and I swallow hard in an effort to erase the feelings that I desperately do not want. Last weekend, he made things crystal clear. And I don't know what I've even been thinking, wanting it to be more than what it is. Who am I kidding?

Delilah is in a situation which is exactly what I try to avoid. I don't want to be involved in any shit like she is, and things with Cam would just be a goddamn mess. A headache that I don't need. It's easier if we're just friends. Just friends don't hand their hearts over to the other to get broken. And with a guy like Cameron Sawyer... there's no way you get involved and make it out with your heart still intact.

"Aspen?" Delilah looks at me expectantly, her

head tilted to the side as her eyebrows pull together. "You didn't hear a single word I said, did you?"

A heat creeps up my neck, spreading across my cheeks as I give her an apologetic smile and a shrug. Delilah's face transforms, a look of suspicion growing in her eyes as the corners of her lips curl upward into a smirk.

"You were thinking about him, weren't you?"

Panic wells inside me and I shake my head. "What? No. There's nothing to think about. There's literally nothing going on between the two of us."

"Uh-huh, right," she says, rolling her eyes with that stupid smirk still glued to her lips. "I saw the two of you together last weekend. Cam and Hayden weren't supposed to play against us in beer pong, but he made such a fuss until the other guys gave up their turn for them to play. Why do you think that is?"

I swallow hard over the knives in my throat. "Because they wanted to be able to play next?"

Delilah shakes her head at me. "Because Cam wanted to play you. Girl, you're blind if you didn't see the way he was watching you the entire time. And don't even fuck with me because I saw the two of you go out back. Not to mention, he walked you to your car then too…"

"The only reason he walked me to my car was because you were preoccupied with Alexander and I was in no condition to drive. Thankfully, Cam wasn't drunk, so he was able to drive me back to my apartment."

"How do you explain the little interaction between the two of you during the game and then sneaking off with him outside?"

I stare back at Delilah, feeling the anxiety building in the pit of my stomach. There's no malice in her tone or any judgement in her expression. I wouldn't expect such things from my best friend, but with the way she's questioning me, I can't help but feel like I'm being interrogated right now.

"I don't even know," I tell her, the lie tasting bitter on my tongue. "I was drunk and needed to get some fresh air, so he was the one who suggested going outside. Nothing happened between us and then we left, to which he drove me back to my apartment and left instead of coming inside." Pausing, I narrow my eyes at her. "Why are you questioning me like this?"

"It's just weird... you give him the cold shoulder at school, but I've seen the two of you in the library together. Not to mention your little study sessions in the evenings during the week." She takes a deep breath, her expression tormented. "I know you have a strict policy of not getting close to anyone, but you've been spending a lot of time with him and it concerns me."

Swallowing hard over the knives lodged in my throat, I stare back at her. I haven't been fully truthful with her and she doesn't know about our tutoring arrangement, but that's because it's not my business to tell. Cam specifically asked me to not tell anyone, so I couldn't bring myself to tell her the truth. Instead, I just told her that we've been studying together.

She's been more observant than I've realized and I'm not sure how I feel about it.

"Why would you be concerned?" I question her, my voice off-kilter as I speak the words. "If anything, we're just friends... and even that is a stretch. I barely know the guy."

"Just be careful with him," she says quietly, her eyes soft and warm as they search mine. "Cam is known to be a player and I would hate to see you get hurt by him."

Narrowing my eyes at her, I grab my drink from the coffee table and unscrew the lid. "What part of just friends are you missing here?"

"I mean, let's be real. Do friendships really work

between two people who are attracted to each other?"

The heat is instant as it spreads across my cheeks and I quickly divert my gaze back to the TV in an effort to avoid her eyes. "While I can appreciate that Cam is attractive, I'm not attracted to him. Trust me. I know enough about him to know that he's not someone to get involved with. Plus, when have I ever been the person to get attached?"

Looking back over at Delilah, she shrugs. "I know you don't get attached, but you don't usually spend this much time with other people, so there's no way for them to ever get close enough to you." She pauses for a moment, her lips curling upward as she picks her spoon up. "And, girl, you're only lying to yourself if you say you're not attracted to him."

"Since when did this conversation turn into grilling me about my friendship with Cam instead of the shit going on between you and Alexander?" I ask her, a light laugh falling from my lips as I nestle into the couch and click the button on the remote to select a movie.

Delilah chuckles, shaking her head. "Because the shit between Alexander and I is pretty fucking black and white... this shit between you and Cam falls into the gray category."

"Oh please," I groan, grabbing a pillow as I whip it over at her. Delilah blocks it with her hand and it falls onto the floor beside the couch. Grabbing a blanket, I cover myself up before looking back over at her. "Cam and I are just friends. Nothing more —ever."

"Yeah, sure." She rolls her eyes in exaggeration and settles on the other part of the sectional she's sitting on. "Talk to me after he crawls under your skin."

"There is no way in hell that is going to happen in this lifetime."

Delilah raises an eyebrow at me. "We'll see," she muses, as she turns her attention back to the ice cream in her lap and the movie playing on the TV.

Ignoring her comment, I turn away from her, my eyes trained on the movie, but I'm not actually focusing on anything that is going on in it. She's got it all wrong if she thinks that I'll be letting Cameron Sawyer in. The last place he is crawling is under my skin.

I don't catch feelings and neither does Cam.

CHAPTER ELEVEN
CAMERON

The ice is where I really feel like I'm at home. Like I have a purpose and am doing the one thing I was put on this earth to do. I know being an athlete isn't exactly a noble act or anything that is life-changing, but it can be inspiring to people. And I know that feeling I felt as a young kid when I fell in love with the sport.

I was the underdog in a way. My parents worked their asses off, saving and scraping extra money together to put me through all of my years playing hockey. Equipment wasn't cheap, skates were fucking expensive, and ice time was never free. The two of them spent tens of thousands of dollars to get me where I am now.

And if it weren't for the full-ride scholarship that

I earned, I don't know that I would even be in the position I'm in now. The professional league comes after this, but if I don't get my shit together, all of that could easily go away.

I can't fuck this up...

And I'm not going to think with my dick and ruin my friendship with Aspen because of it.

Skating across the ice, I effortlessly move the puck along with my stick, moving past Logan as he attempts to get it away from me. He mutters a curse under his breath and a smile creeps onto my lips as I pass the puck to August who takes his shot at our second-string goalie. He flicks his wrists, shooting the puck in the top shelf, and Bishop doesn't stand a chance at stopping the goal.

Since we have the regional tournament starting, we've been fitting in scrimmage games at the end of practice. Even though we're still in the season and playing on the weekends, it feels good playing against my guys and seeing their skills really shine.

By the time we finish up, I score the last goal that puts us in the lead after being tied for a decent amount of time. Everyone's sweaty and fucking exhausted as we leave the ice and head back to the locker room. It's already well into the evening and we all have to be back here tomorrow afternoon for a game.

As I step inside the locker room, I drop my gloves onto the bench and unsnap my helmet before pulling it off my head. My hair is damp with sweat and my chest heaves, still trying to catch my breath after skating my ass off. I shouldn't have gone as hard as I did tonight, but it's a welcomed distraction from everything else in life.

I chase that adrenaline like a junkie chasing their next high.

Hockey is the most important thing in my life and on the rare occasion, I have to remind myself of that. To keep myself focused and my head in the game. I'm so close to reaching my end goal and I can't let anything get in the way of that now.

"What are you getting into tonight?" Hayden asks me as he drops down onto the bench next to me and begins to unlace his skates. He's only been here for a month or so now and most of the guys have taken him under their wing as if he's always been one of their own.

The thing with Hayden, though, is he really has been one of us. Logan, August, Hayden, and I all grew up together, playing together. We've always had an unbreakable bond and I think that helped

when he transferred schools and started playing
college hockey on our team. Throughout the years,
we've played against him, but it was nice having
him on our side now.

Hayden had every intention of coming to
Wyncote with us. If you were going to play college
hockey and wanted the professional scouts to see
you, Wyncote was exactly where you wanted to be.
Hayden's parents had other plans for him and
insisted that he went to the same Ivy League school
that his father went to, especially because they had
dreams of him following in his father's footsteps
and becoming a lawyer.

That would never be Hayden and it was never
what he wanted. Maybe he did what he did as a way
to get out of where he was. Even though we all share
so much with each other, there's still parts of
Hayden that you just can't get to. That kid's like a
fucking vault and he'll only let you in if he feels like
it's necessary.

"I think I'm just going to go home and sleep," I
tell him, my voice exhausted and honest. "Seriously.
We've been going hard at practice and I can feel it in
my legs right now."

"Come on, man," he groans as he pulls his practice jersey over his head. "Some of us are going out

to the bar. I think old man Logan is even coming and bringing Isla with him."

Logan shouts some obscenities at him from across the locker room, cutting his eyes at him in annoyance. If I'm being honest, there are times that I feel bad for Logan. He gets a lot of shit from everyone because of being tied down like he is now. Personally, I couldn't be happier for him. This is the first time I've seen Logan truly happy and I'm sure it's because he doesn't have to keep things between them a secret anymore.

"What about you, August?" I question him as he shoves his gear into his bag. He's already dressed in a pair of sweatpants and sweatshirt, his hair still damp with sweat instead of water from the shower. That's a telltale sign that he's heading out.

"I don't know, man." His voice is strained and I know he has a lot going on right now too. Poppy's pregnant with his baby and things aren't good between them. They weren't in a relationship when it happened, but I know that he's been struggling with the way things are.

"Dude, just come out," Hayden urges him, a hopeful look in his eye. "You said it yourself that Poppy needs space, so what is going home and being depressed going to do? You need to get your mind off shit and just blow off some steam."

August shrugs at him. "Maybe I will. Either way, I want to go home and shower and change first."

Hayden nods, grabbing his clothes before he heads over to the shower. "You know where to find us if you decide you want to come out."

————

I end up at the bar with Hayden, Asher, Sterling, and Simon. We grabbed one of the high-top tables and have already had two rounds of beer. Logan and August never ended up showing up, which wasn't surprising. I can't say I really blame them, because there are times where this shit begins to feel like it's getting old.

Like there has to be something else out there that is more fulfilling...

But I'm not like the two of them. I will never be built for a relationship.

Asher, Sterling, and Simon are all caught up in an argument about some of the goals from earlier tonight. I can feel Hayden's gaze on the side of my face and after ignoring it for a few moments, I finally turn my head to look at him.

"What?" I ask him, picking up my beer to take a swig of it.

"What happened with your girl last weekend? We never really got a chance to talk about it since you were so damn silent the entire car ride back after dropping her car off."

My stomach sinks at the thought of that night and how awkward things have been between us since then. "She's not my girl," I mumble, rolling my eyes at him.

Hayden raises an eyebrow at me with a look of amusement dancing in his eyes. "Are you sure about that?"

"Bro, she's just a friend. We have some classes together and have been hanging out to study. That's literally it."

I watch him as he nods, lifting his beer to his lips as he drains the rest of the cup. "Whatever you say, man," he offers, shrugging in defeat. "I'm not going to argue when you're still lying to yourself about it all, but I'm going to call it now. Logan and August are already wrapped up in their chicks. You're definitely the next one to go."

A harsh laugh falls from my lips and I shake my head at him. "Not a chance, King. I will never be more than friends with Aspen. I don't do relationship shit and I have no intention of fucking up our friendship by trying to make a move on her."

"So, if you're not going to make a move on her, then she's fair game, right?" Hayden smirks, a sinister look passing through his irises.

My grip tightens around my glass of beer and my jaw clenches. Anger radiates through me at the mere thought of Hayden and Aspen. My blood boils, my stomach recoiling as I narrow my eyes at him. There's a coldness in my gaze and I watch as Hayden's face relaxes, a soft laugh falling from his lips.

"Exactly what I thought." He smiles, shaking his head as he grabs the pitcher from the center of the table and rises to his feet. "When you're done lying to yourself about your feelings for her, let me know."

I watch him as he heads over to the bar to get the pitcher refilled and my heart is clawing at my rib cage. He's wrong. Sure, I'm attracted to Aspen, but I know it can't go any further than that.

And I refuse to let that ever happen...

CHAPTER TWELVE
ASPEN

"Are you sure all of this makes sense?" I ask Cam as he sits next to me, his eyes lifting to meet mine.

He nods eagerly, showing me the notes he took while I was explaining all of the material to him. "The way you broke it down makes so much more sense than how Professor McDavid was explaining it in class. You want to try some of the practice questions if you don't believe me?"

A smile touches my lips and I shake my head at him, feeling a sense of pride. We've been having these tutoring sessions for a few weeks now, and even though we had a minor hiccup with where we stood at the beginning, things have been going really well. Cameron isn't stupid and is actually fairly smart. His brain just works a little differently when it comes to understanding the material that we're learning.

And I think that the one-on-one sessions have really been helping him.

"Do you think you're ready for the exam tomorrow morning?" I question him, flipping the page in my notebook to a fresh one.

Cameron's eyes bounce back and forth between mine. "Do you think I am?"

"Of course," I tell him honestly, nodding eagerly at him. "You seem to have all of this practically memorized, which is amazing. I'm beginning to wonder if this was all just a ploy to get me to hang out with you when you already know all of the material. Are you sure you even need me?"

His eyes widen slightly, his throat bobbing as he swallows hard. His expression is unreadable for a moment, but he quickly recovers as a smirk plays on his lips. "Shit, Rossi. You're onto me, aren't you?" He pauses for a second, a soft laugh falling from his lips before he stares directly at me. "I'm kidding. There is literally no way I would be able to pass this shit without you. You've literally been a godsend, Aspen. Seriously... I don't know how I will ever be able to repay you for this."

Cameron's voice is like silk, sliding across my eardrums as I get lost in the storm that brews in his irises. There's something about him that has me captivated. In his presence, it's like nothing else around us even matters. I'm drawn to him like a moth to a flame and as much as I hate it, I love it.

I know that he's mainly all talk and I accept it as that because this will never go any further than friendship. But I would be lying if I said he didn't make me feel good... because he does.

"You don't have to repay me, Cam," I tell him, my voice soft as I search his eyes. "Like I said, I can put it on my résumé. And when you make it to the NHL, just get me some amazing seats to a game and we can call this even."

Lifting his arm onto the table, he rests his elbow on the wooden surface and props his chin on his hand as he tilts his head to the side. "You like hockey?"

"I've never really watched it, to be honest. But it would be pretty cool to go to a game and be able to say that my friend is playing on that team."

Cameron stares at me for a moment. "Would you want to come to one of my games sometime?" His voice is soft, his words strained for a moment, but he covers it up with a nervous chuckle. "I mean,

I know it isn't a professional game, but it's still a hockey game."

A smile creeps onto my lips and I nod at him, watching the anxiety drain from his face as he visibly relaxes. "I would love to."

His smile touches his eyes and they shine brightly at me. No words fall from his lips, but instead we fall into a silence as he stares at me for a moment. I'm lost in the depths of his stormy green eyes. Even when he isn't in a bad mood, there's still a darkness lurking in them, but I can't quite put my finger on it.

But it's a darkness that I want to explore.

I don't want to get involved with him, but I want to know his secrets. There's an air of mystery to him, mainly because he isn't as much of an open book like people think. He keeps everything superficial and at face value. He's charming and he knows how to use it to his advantage without letting anyone get close to him.

The more time we spend together, I can't help but feel like I'm inching closer to the pieces of him that he keeps hidden from the rest of the world.

Cameron's eyes fall down to my lips and linger there for a moment. My heart pounds erratically in my chest as he inches closer to me, his hand reaching out as he brushes a stray hair away from my face. His fingertips are soft on my skin, a shiver climbing up my spine from his touch. I hate the effect he has on me, but I allow myself to feel it—to revel in it.

If only just for a moment...

He tucks the hair behind my ear, slowly trailing his fingers down the side of my face as he inches closer to me. Just as I think he's about to kiss me, he pauses. He's so fucking close, his breath is warm against my lips, but he doesn't dare to bring his mouth to mine.

"I'm starving," he murmurs, trailing his fingertips down the side of my neck. "Do you want to go get dinner with me?"

My throat bobs as I swallow hard, my breath caught in my throat as I stare up at him. His breath smells like cotton candy and I want to taste it on his tongue. Drawing my bottom lip between my teeth, I bite down and nod, not fully trusting my voice.

"There's an Italian restaurant that I heard is really good. Let me take you out, as a way to say thank you?"

"Okay," I whisper, my heart rattling in its cage as my breathing grows shallow. Cam slowly pulls his hand away from me before leaning back.

I expect his typical playful smirk, but it isn't there. Instead, he stares at me with a heated gaze— one that is almost identical to the one he had the night that he told me I was breathtaking.

This is a line that we cannot cross, regardless of how tempting it might be.

Cameron Sawyer is the biggest temptation in my life and I don't know how much longer I'll be able to fight against these feelings.

Perhaps if I just allow myself a small taste, I can get him out of my system.

And with the way he's looking at me right now, I'm beginning to wonder if food is really what he's hungry for...

CHAPTER THIRTEEN
CAMERON

Fuck. What am I doing?

I need to stop letting these moments happen between us. Each and every time, I get so fucking caught up, and I can't help myself from toeing that dangerous line. Aspen already made things clear and I voiced my stance on it. We have to remain as just friends. Crossing that line could fuck this all up.

Unless there was a way around it. We could still be friends. Friends with benefits. And if it doesn't work out, we just go back to the way things are. As long as feelings don't get involved. I don't have to worry about that for myself, but it's her that concerns me. I know Aspen doesn't seem to develop attachments, but I'd hate for her to do that with me.

Especially when I would never be able to recip-rocate that.

Friends with benefits is beginning to sound more enticing as I mull over the idea of it in the car. Aspen is fairly silent, toying with Bluetooth settings in my car as she attempts to connect her phone to it. She's said a few things, but with the pink tint that hasn't left her cheeks and the way she shifts nervously in her seat, I know she's just as affected by the tension as I am.

Sexual tension is the fucking worst, especially when you don't know how to eradicate it. I think I may have our solution, though—but it will only work if Aspen agrees to it with the same mindset that I have about it.

Aspen finally connects her phone just as we're pulling up to the restaurant. It wasn't a far drive from campus, but with the way things feel between us right now, the car felt like it was suffocating me. I need to get out, get some fresh air, and tell my dick that he needs to behave.

I find a parking spot and turn off the engine as Aspen climbs out on her side. She doesn't even give me the chance to walk around to help her out, but I attempt to make up for it as I hold the door open for her to walk into the restaurant. As we step inside, the place is packed and since I forgot to put in our name ahead of time, the hostess tells me that it's going to be at least an hour wait.

"Do you want to go somewhere else?" I ask Aspen as we walk back through the doors, stepping into the chill of the night. There was barely any standing room inside to wait, so we had no option but to come out here.

Aspen shrugs, a smile touching her lips. "I'm honestly not a picky eater at all," she tells me, glancing back at the restaurant. "If you don't want to wait, we can definitely go somewhere else."

I'm a little annoyed at the fact that the restaurant is packed, since I wanted somewhere quiet for the two of us to eat and talk. Considering the fact that it's a Friday night, I think our chances of finding a place like this are slim unless we want to wait or call ahead.

"There's a sports bar not far from here," I offer. "It's where we usually go after practice or a game. They have good food there and there's also the restaurant area if you don't want to sit in the bar section."

Aspen smiles up at me, wrapping her arms around her middle to shield herself from the cold breeze. "That sounds perfect to me. Anywhere we can get a seat and something to eat."

Smiling back at her, I fight the urge to wrap my arms around her to keep her warm and instead turn back toward the parking lot. She follows along behind me, her shorter stride extending to keep up with my long legs. I slow down my pace, stopping at the passenger's side as I open the door for her.

Thanking me, Aspen drops down into her seat and I wait until she's tucked inside before shutting the door. My mind is reeling as I round the front of the car. Perhaps this was a bad idea and I shouldn't have brought her out with me.

It's too late for that now...

———

The bar is pretty crowded when we get there, but we're able to grab a high-top table on the opposite side of the room. Aspen seems pretty content with it, not bothered by anything going on. I know that she doesn't really drink much, but she seems to fit in with the atmosphere. In a way, she's like a chameleon. Constantly changing to fit the mold of whatever environment she is in.

It's not that she doesn't belong anywhere she

goes. She spends so much time in her own head, it's like she's trained herself to just adapt and conform to whatever she needs to. I'm not sure if I like it or hate it. Her mood or behavior toward me doesn't change, but there's a shift. Like her guard is back in place and I want to tear it down and break it to pieces.

"Do you know what you want to eat?" I ask her as I set my menu down. I ordered myself a beer and Aspen stayed true to herself, ordering a water instead. Maybe I was wrong about her need to conform to her environment. Perhaps she's just being herself and is actually that laid-back and easy-going with whatever atmosphere she is in. If she were trying to fit in, I feel like she would have ordered an alcoholic drink too.

I don't know what it is about her, but I cannot fucking figure her out.

Just when I think I've opened a door inside her, I'm met with another closed door. She's more complex than she lets on. Fucking layered as hell, and I'm ready to peel her layers away.

"Yep," she says easily, just as our server, Amanda, walks over to the table. She's been working here for as long as we've been coming here. I didn't miss the disapproval in Aspen's expression when

Amanda greeted me by name. I come here too often, clearly.

Surprisingly, none of the guys are here. They were all talking about going out when I last saw them, but maybe they decided to try somewhere new. Of course, none of them let up on the shit they were giving me when they found out I was studying with Aspen. If any of them saw us here tonight, they would be fucking eating it up.

Aspen goes ahead and places her order before I tell Amanda what I want too. She writes down our food order and then disappears from the table into the crowded bar. There's a playoff game on the TVs here, so most of the patrons are all drinking and watching the game, which reminds me of Aspen's confession earlier.

"So, you said you wanted to come to one of my games?" I ask her, having to raise my voice as the crowd cheers for the team that scored. "Do you know Isla, August's sister?"

Aspen nods, lifting her glass of water to her lips as she takes a sip. I watch her slender throat, the way it moves as she swallows the cold liquid. "Yeah, I have a class with her. We don't really talk much, but she seems nice enough. She's dating Logan Knight, right?"

"Yeah. She usually comes to most of the games and we always have a few open seats that are reserved for friends and family." I watch her as her tongue darts out, slowly licking her lips before she parts them slightly. "If you want, I can have her call you if you guys want to sit together."

"That would be nice," she says softly, a smile touching her plump lips. "You don't think she would mind if I sat with her, do you? If not, I could always just get tickets to the game or something."

"Nonsense," I retort, shaking my head at her. She isn't my girl, but the last thing I'm going to do is let her buy tickets to come to my game. If she's coming, she sits where we have seats reserved. "Just let me know when you want to come to one and I'll have everything arranged."

Aspen smiles back at me, her lips parting as she goes to respond, but I watch as she quickly closes them. Her face falls for a moment, her eyebrows pulling together as she looks just over my shoulder. And then I feel a pair of hands touching my back, the sensation of long fake nails pressing against my skin.

"Hey you," Kiara breathes in my ear, the smell of liquor flooding my senses as she leans against my back. "Who do you have with you?"

My eyes lift to Aspen's and she raises a suspicious eyebrow as I silently apologize to her with my gaze. "This is Aspen," I tell Kiara, wishing that she would just fucking disappear.

Kiara is a barfly that I met here last year. She isn't an ex, but she's someone I fucked around with more times than I wanted to admit. Things were never serious between the two of us and we never had a relationship, but I've been to her apartment enough times to spark some jealousy in her.

Plus, this isn't the first time she's tried to chase another girl away. Although, none of them were like Aspen. I didn't care if she chased them away, because she always had a bed for me to land in. Things are different with Aspen, though, and the last thing I need is an old fuck buddy running her off.

Because the last place I was going was home with Kiara.

"Aspen," Kiara slurs and Aspen's name on her tongue sounds fucking wrong. "What a pretty name. Only seems fitting for such a pretty girl too. I'm Kiara," she says, holding her hand out to shake it.

Aspen quickly recovers, shielding the suspicious look on her face as she offers Kiara a warm smile. Taking her hand, she shakes it before dropping it like it's contaminated with germs. "It's nice to meet you," she offers softly, with no malice detected in her voice.

Her eyes slice back to my gaze and I don't miss the coldness that settles in them as Kiara stands beside me, her hand still on my shoulder.

"I haven't heard from you in a while," Kiara tells me, her bloodshot eyes searching mine. "I thought that maybe I did something wrong, but now it all makes sense. This isn't the first time I've seen you with another girl, but this one is different, isn't she?"

I swallow hard, my jaw clenching as I narrow my eyes at Kiara. "It was nice seeing you, Kiara, but I haven't called you because I moved on. You know how things go."

"Mhm," she murmurs, dragging the sharp tip of her long nail down the side of my neck. "I also know that I'm the one you always come back to."

Aspen clears her throat and Kiara looks back to her, tilting her head to the side. "Is there something wrong, honey?"

My jaw feels like it's going to lock up with how tight it is right now. I stare back at Aspen who looks like she could potentially be sick as I plead with her using my eyes. "You need to leave, Kiara," I tell her as Aspen rises to her feet. "Where are you going?" I question her, pushing Kiara's hand away from me.

"I need to use the restroom," she says quietly, the hurt lingering in her eyes as she quickly diverts her gaze toward the floor.

Aspen starts to move through the crowd and I'm right behind her, leaving Kiara standing back at the table. "Aspen, hold on!" I call after her, following her into the hallway that leads to the bathrooms.

She stops, spinning on her heel as her gaze meets mine with a look of torment. "What, Cameron? Clearly, this was a mistake. You could have at least told me that your girlfriend or whatever the hell she is would be here."

"She's not my girlfriend and I didn't know she would be here," I tell her with nothing but honesty as I chance a step toward her. Aspen takes a step away from me, backing up until her back hits the wall. Following along with her, I plant my palms on either side of her head as I stare down at her. "Are you jealous, Aspen?"

Her throat bobs as she swallows hard. "Absolutely not. I don't care what you do or who you do it with."

"Oh yeah?" I question her, tilting my head to the side as I lift an eyebrow. "So, if I were to go home with Kiara tonight, you wouldn't give a shit, would you?"

Aspen's jaw tics and she shakes her head as she lifts her chin in defiance. "Nope. Do whatever the hell you want, Cam. You're a grown-ass man and we're just friends, remember?"

A smirk falls on my lips and my face dips down to hers, breathing in her soft floral scent. Aspen's lips part slightly, a ragged breath falling from her as her chest rises and falls in rapid succession. "Just friends... I'm not sure how I feel about that anymore, babe."

"Then do something about it."

CHAPTER FOURTEEN
ASPEN

Cam stares down at me, a glimmer of mischief shining in his bright green eyes. With one hand planted on the wall beside my head, he brings the other to the side of my face. His palm warms my skin, his fingertips gently caressing my cheek. His lips lightly brush against mine and my eyelids flutter shut.

His mouth collides with mine, inhaling me in one swift breath. Reaching for him, my hands find his waist and I pull him closer as his tongue slides along the seam of my lips. Parting them, I let him in, his tongue tangling with mine as we're caught up in the moment.

Cam slips his hands into my hair, holding me to him as he consumes me. His lips are soft, moving against mine as we toe the line of our friendship. None of that matters in this moment. The only thing that matters is feeling his firm body pressed against mine, like it's exactly where he belongs.

My fingertips dig into his flesh and his cock is rock hard as he rolls his hips, pressing it into my stomach. With our height difference, my neck is straining and fully exposed with my head tipped back. Cam doesn't stop, his touch gentle, and I taste a hint of beer on his tongue as it dances with mine.

I can't breathe and I'm completely okay with that. I've never wanted to drown in someone as badly as I do right now and I'm ready to dive into his depths.

A door slams in the distance and someone snickers as they walk past us. The moment is ruined and my heart pounds erratically in my chest, knowing we've been seen.

Cam slowly pulls away, my lips parting as I suck in a shallow breath. He presses his forehead to mine, his chest rapidly rising and falling. We both come up for air and I'm not ready for it. I instantly feel his absence and I'm brought back to reality in a rush.

Shit. We crossed a line that wasn't meant to be crossed.

Neither of us say a word as he slowly releases me

and takes a step backward. A warmth creeps up my neck, spreading across my cheeks as I feel the mark he left on me. Lust runs rampant through my veins and I feel it pooling in the pit of my stomach. If we weren't in public right now, I'm afraid to think about how far we would have really gone.

"I'm sorry," I let out a rush of air, my words breathless. "I—" I pause, the words getting caught in my throat. I don't even know what I'm really apologizing for here. For the jealousy I was feeling when I saw him with another girl? For challenging him when he said about us being friends?

"Aspen, stop," he breathes, stepping back toward me as he cups the sides of my face. His eyes desperately search mine, laced with lust and guilt. "I was the one who made the move. You didn't do anything wrong."

Swallowing hard, I stare back at him. My heart violently thrashes in its cage. "Can we just forget about this and pretend it never happened?"

A chuckle vibrates in Cam's chest and he raises an eyebrow at me. "If that's what you want, babe." He pauses for a moment, dropping his face down to mine. His breath is warm against my lips, but he doesn't kiss me. "We can pretend, but I don't think either of us can forget."

My breath catches in my throat as he pulls away from me, his hands leaving the sides of my face as he tucks them in the front pockets of his pants. A storm brews in his eyes as he stares directly through me and a contradicting smirk plays on his lips.

"I'll be waiting for you at the table."

Standing with my back still against the wall, I nod, not fully trusting my voice. Cam gives me one last glance before he spins on his heel and strolls down the hallway, stepping back into the bar area. Letting out the breath I didn't realize I was still holding, I head in the opposite direction, locking myself away in the bathroom as I get myself together.

After using the bathroom, I wash my hands and find myself lingering by the sink. My hands grip the countertop as I stare at myself in the mirror. My hair is slightly tousled, my lips plump and bright red from his against mine. Lifting my fingertips to my mouth, I press them against my flesh, still wanting to feel him against me.

I can't let my mind go down this road. The last place that Cameron Sawyer is going to be is under my skin. We crossed a line and it's not one that we can cross again. Friends don't kiss friends like that.

And I'll be damned if I get involved with the playboy jock.

My face is still flushed, no doubt from the effect he has on me. I let thoughts of Kiara wander back into my head. I don't want the jealousy from it, but I want the reminder—even if it is painful. I'm just as disposable to Cameron as the other girls before me were. And messing around with him goes against all of my standards.

Although, perhaps if we kept our feelings out of this, we wouldn't necessarily be crossing a line. We can still be friends and fuck around without getting caught up in something more than that. Cam is using me to help him get through the rest of the year and bring his grades up. It's only right that I get something in return.

Perhaps it's time to take him up on that offer of repaying me.

And we could both benefit from this proposition... as long as we keep any feelings and emotions out of it. We could be friends with benefits and leave it at that. After the semester is over, we go our separate ways like none of this had ever happened. There's no room for either of us in each other's lives, since we both have our plans that we're sticking to.

But in the meantime, Cam could help me pass the time.

As long as he doesn't become a distraction, because then I would have to end everything between us. Our tutoring arrangement and friendship.

After collecting myself, I head back out of the bathroom. As I walk down the hall, part of me wishes that Kiara is back at the table. If Cam were still involved with her, it would be easier to separate myself and completely detach. Friends with benefits wouldn't even be an option. But as I walk back to the table and find him by himself, I'm torn between an elated feeling and swirling disappointment.

Cam's gaze meets mine, a ghost of a smile playing on his lips as I sit down in my seat. He lifts his beer to his lips and my eyes are instantly drawn to them, watching as he swallows down some of the amber-colored liquid. His eyes never leave mine, staring directly at me as he sets the glass back down.

"Where's your little friend?" I ask him, keeping any emotion from my voice as I picture her hand on his shoulder again.

A soft chuckle slips from his lips as he tips his head toward the bar. "She found someone else to bother."

Glancing over toward the bar, I see Kiara with another guy and it looks like she's fully immersed in the conversation they're having, completely forgetting about Cameron. It brings me a sense of peace it shouldn't and my heart all but crawls into my throat.

Swallowing it back down, I grab my water and quickly gulp some of it down as I look back to Cam. Our server shows back up, setting our food in front of us, and I welcome the distraction. As I toy with my food on my plate, I can't help but look at Cameron as he pops a fry into his mouth.

"You know how you said about paying me back for tutoring you?" I start, my voice sounding more confident than I actually feel. My stomach rolls with anxiety and my heart hammers against my rib cage. "I changed my mind. There is a way you can pay me back..."

Cam tilts his head to the side. "Oh yeah? What did you have in mind?"

"I don't want to pretend like what happened in the hallway didn't. I also still want to be friends with you and nothing more."

"Hmm," he muses, the corners of his lips lifting. "Well, it sounds like you're caught in quite the predicament. Wanting to have your cake and eat it too."

I swallow hard over the nervousness that builds inside. "I was hoping maybe you could help me with this problem. We've already crossed a line, but I think there may be a loophole when it comes to crossing it again."

"Enlighten me, baby," he breathes, a smirk on his lips as his bright eyes search mine.

"Friends with benefits. We don't get any more involved than that and at the end of the semester, we go our separate ways."

It feels like a weight has been lifted as soon as the words leave my lips, but I want the ground to open up and swallow me whole as I'm caught under Cam's watchful eye.

"So, we get to cross the line as long as we keep it that we're just friends?" There's a lilt in his voice and a smile touches my lips. "No strings, no feelings."

"Definitely no feelings," I assure him, nodding as I spear my fork into my salad. "That way we're not restricted and feeling guilty after something happens like in the hallway. We just roll with it, as long as neither of us get attached."

Cam smirks with a sinister gleam in his eyes.

"Trust me, babe. I don't do feelings, so you don't have to worry about any of that shit."

"Do we have a deal?" I ask him, extending my arm for him to take my hand. "No feelings or attachments. Just friends with some added benefits."

Cameron slips his hand into mine, his palm warming my skin as he wraps his fingers around my own, and we shake on it.

"Deal."

CHAPTER FIFTEEN
CAMERON

My skates slide across the ice as I use the power from my legs to move me closer to where the puck is at center ice. August is also staking toward it, but he has one of the other team's defensemen on him. I get to the puck before both of them, out-skating the guy who was following me, and head in the direction of their net. None of the other guys can keep up with me and it's practically open ice as I skate down there.

The goalie drops into a butterfly position as I fake him out. Instead of sending the puck toward his legs, I flick my wrist, sending it soaring into the top shelf. It goes just above the goalie's shoulder and he isn't able to block the shot as it makes its way into the net.

The horn blares in the arena and I can hear other people shouting as the other players on my team start slapping their sticks against the boards. August and Sterling skate over to me, congratulating me as they both knock their gloves against my helmet. The other guys come up to me, all doing the same before everyone begins to skate back.

As I make my way over to the bench and hop the boards, the guys sitting there all congratulate me, too. Logan and Hayden smile through the cages on their helmets and I drop down onto the bench next to Hayden as a shift change happens. There's only about two minutes left in the third period and we're leading with four to one.

Anything can happen in those last few minutes, though.

The game is constantly changing and the more aggressive the players get, it's harder to tell what is going to really happen. Anyone could easily get injured and the last thing we need is for one of our key players to get fucked up. All that we can do in these last two minutes is hope for the fucking best and play our asses off.

Leaning forward in my seat, I watch as the other guys skate around, fighting for the puck against the other team. Since they're losing, they've grown more aggressive. One slashes at Asher's arm as he blocks a shot. The refs miss the slashing and don't call a penalty. Logan jumps to his feet, screaming shift change as he keeps his eyes on the player who hit Asher.

A lot of times, different calls go missed and that's when Logan comes in to take matters into his own hands. He's the enforcer of our team and isn't afraid to throw his gloves and get his hands bloody. Not many of the other guys fight, but they all will if it's necessary. Logan is a special breed of person, though. He's always ready to go to war for the people who are important to him.

The tension is thick in the air and one of our defensive players skates off the ice, hopping over the boards. Logan is already on the ice before Simon even sits down and he's skating toward the center for the face-off. There's nothing I can do from here but sit back and watch until it's my turn to get back out there.

Our shifts aren't very long, since the sport is so fucking physically taxing. I have about ten seconds and then I'll be back on the ice for the remainder of the game. I watch as Hayden switches out and Logan already has the other player cornered.

One of the refs blow the whistle and the play

stops as Logan and the other guy throw their gloves onto the ice, squaring up in front of each other. Jumping onto my skates, I watch with the rest of our team as fists start flying until the other guy ends up lying by Logan's feet. Logan skates over, grabbing his helmet and gloves as he gets a penalty. He shakes his head as he heads into the box, and the other team gets their power play.

During the power play, we're cut down to four players on the ice instead of five, so by the time it's my turn, there's only fifteen seconds left in the game. The other team doesn't stand a chance against Asher, who's even more pissed off than he was before. He blocks their last shot and the buzzer goes off as we reach the end of the game.

Another win in the books and we're down to a few short weeks left until regionals. Everyone congratulates each other, skating back to the bench before we all head down the tunnel toward the locker room. The guys are in great spirits and it's the energy I fucking need. I live for this shit and we're all riding on the adrenaline and the high of our victory.

Dropping down onto the bench in the locker room, I strip out of my gear and take off my skates before shoving everything into my bag. A bunch of the guys head over to get showered, and Logan stands by the mirror as he blots the cut above his eyebrow. Walking past him, I clutch my stuff to head for the shower room and pause behind him for a moment.

"Damn, I didn't realize that he got you," I tell him, leaning against the wall as August comes strolling back from the showers. He stops beside me, narrowing his eyes at Logan through the mirror.

"Yeah, he packed a harder punch than I expected," he responds to me before looking at August through the mirror. "And don't you even start. I'm already going to get shit from your sister when I get home."

August chuckles, shaking his head at him. "You would think she'd expect this by now."

"She's never going to get used to her pretty boy getting his face fucked up," Hayden throws in as he strides past the three of us with a smirk. "But seriously. Good fight, Knight. You're always ready to go to bat for each and every one of us, with no questions asked."

"Well, if it really came down to it, I would hope you guys would do the same," Logan retorts.

"If there's one person that I'm not going to bat for you against, it's your girl," Hayden laughs, shaking his head. "That chick scares the shit out of me and she has since we were kids."

"She's harmless," August rolls his eyes. "All bark, no bite."

"Bullshit," Hayden argues as he heads back toward his locker. "That girl has fangs and she's not afraid to use them."

The three of them keep bullshitting as I head over to the showers and slip into the hot water. As I wash my body and scrub off the sweat and hockey smell, my mind drifts back to Aspen. Her proposition was unexpected, but I would have been a fool to turn down an offer like that. Friends with benefits, I can definitely do.

But she needs to understand that I'm the only friend she'll be having benefits with.

After finishing up my shower, I head over to my locker, noticing that most of the guys have already left. Hayden lingers as he wraps fresh tape around the blade of his stick. He lifts his gaze to mine, raising an eyebrow, but he doesn't question me as I pull out my phone.

Instead of texting Aspen, I tap on her name and call her. It rings three times before she picks up and I can barely hear her over the loud music in the background as she answers.

"Hey! Hold on," she breathes, dropping her voice as she speaks to someone in the background. "I'll be right back. It's too loud."

Shifting my weight on my feet, I hold the phone between my shoulder and ear as I put my dirty clothes in my hockey bag. I listen as the noise in the background grows quieter until Aspen's voice is clear when she speaks.

"Sorry about that," she laughs nervously. "Delilah forced me out to this party and it's pretty loud right now."

"Oh yeah?" I question her, my voice colder than I intended. "I was calling to see if you were busy tonight and wanted to hang out."

Hayden snorts and I cut my eyes at him, narrowing them in warning before I continue ignoring him. Clutching my phone in my hand, I listen as Aspen tells me where she's at. Some asshole named Carter's house. Supposedly Delilah knows him from volunteering at the hospital, so that's why I didn't hear about it on campus.

"You should come by," she offers quietly. "I honestly don't really feel like being here. Most of the people here are from Drezel, so I only know Delilah and a few other people she mentioned the party to. It's fucking crowded as shit too."

"You want me to?"

"Please," she breathes softly. "Come save me from this hell."

"Send me the address and I'm on my way, baby."

We end the call and I glance over at Hayden as Aspen shares her location with me. I click on the address, having the directions show up. "You wanna go to a party?" I ask Hayden, who is staring at me with curiosity.

His lips curl upward. "When do I ever say no?"

"Get your shit together, so we can go."

Hayden raises an eyebrow at me. "Are we going to ignore the fact that you called her baby?"

"Yep," I answer him curtly, as I zip up my bag. "You got five minutes if you're coming along. I'll be waiting in my car."

Leaving Hayden in the locker room, I head out to my car and throw my stuff in the trunk before sliding in behind the wheel. Hayden doesn't take that long and puts his stuff in his car before striding over to mine. He hops in the passenger seat and it isn't long before we're on the road, heading in the direction of where Aspen is.

I don't know what the hell I'm getting myself into tonight, but hopefully it's Aspen...

CHAPTER SIXTEEN
ASPEN

I'm pretty positive that I'm the only sober person at this party right now. Delilah invited me along and I thought it was worth attempting to get out of the house for the night. Now that I'm here, I honestly wish I wouldn't have even bothered. Delilah has been working part-time at the local hospital and one of the guys she met invited us here.

There isn't a single person I recognize here, but Delilah doesn't seem to mind. She introduced me to a few of her friends from work. This is the first time she's hung out with any of them outside of work and with the way she's hanging all over Carter, I can see that she has ulterior motives.

After things didn't work out with Alexander and

she pretty much told him to get lost, it didn't take her long to move on to the next guy that showed her some fraction of attention. I can't say I fully blame her for it. Delilah craves male attention, probably from her lack of having a father present in her life.

And honestly... sometimes that attention is nice for anyone. Delilah's only problem is she usually falls quickly and when she does, she falls hard. And after everything comes crashing down, I'm the only one who is there to piece her back together again.

Delilah saunters over to me as I drop down onto an empty spot on the couch. "You look miserable," she slurs, her eyebrows tugging together in disapproval. "Did you want to leave? I can see if one of the guys can give you a ride." She calls out to someone named Leo and waves him over.

I shake my head at her. "I'm pretty sure no one is really in any condition to drive right now."

Leo walks over to us, looking like he stepped right off the front of a GQ magazine. He smiles at me, revealing perfect teeth that only money can buy. "Hey, I'm Leo," he says, extending his arm for me to shake his hand.

"Aspen," I tell him, slicing my eyes to Delilah's as she shrugs. "I don't need a ride."

Leo drops down onto the couch beside me, his cologne overwhelming my senses. Delilah lifts her eyebrows at me, a smirk playing on her lips before she winks and leaves the two of us alone. I'm uncomfortable next to him and shift my weight nervously as he takes a sip of whatever is in his plastic cup.

"So, are you pre-med too?" he asks me, his gray eyes burning with curiosity as he turns to face me. "I know Delilah from the hospital. I'm finishing up my first year of med school this year."

My eyes widen, my curiosity piqued. "Yeah, I am. What specialty are you interested in?"

Leo smiles, taking another sip of his drink. "I want to be an orthopedic surgeon, but I plan on exploring my other options before completely committing." His eyes search mine, a fire burning in his irises. "Have you decided on where you want to go to med school yet? You know Drezel is one of the best in the nation and it's not that far from Wyncote..."

"I've thought about Drezel," I tell him honestly. It's one of my top three dream schools, but I know that admission is extremely competitive. It's hard to get my hopes up and have my sights settled on one school when I know how hard it can be to get in.

"It's in my top three. I'm obviously going to apply to others just in case."

"Hey, don't sell yourself short already." He smiles at me, wrapping his arm around the back of the couch. He doesn't touch me but I can feel his warmth with how close he is and it makes me uncomfortable. Not because there's anything wrong with him. I've known him for two seconds, but the last thing he gives off is creepy vibes. It just feels wrong because he's not Cam. "If you ever want to come tour the campus or anything, let me know. I'd be more than happy to show you around."

"You don't even know me," I remind him, tilting my head to the side as I raise an eyebrow. "What makes you so sure that I even have a chance of getting into Drezel?"

Leo blinks, his steel gray eyes shining back at me. His gaze drops down to the water bottle that I'm clutching in my hands before his gaze meets mine again with a hint of amusement playing in his expression. "I'm usually a good judge of character. I'm not often wrong about people and you don't really strike me as the type of girl who came to college to party and fuck around. Right or wrong?"

My lips part as I smile back at him, a soft chuckle falling from my lips. "You're right. My sole focus right now is my classes. Not to brag, but I'm currently on track to graduating with honors."

He narrows his eyes playfully, a chuckle vibrating from his chest. "And you're actually worried about med school? Shit, I'm pretty positive you could probably get into the school of your choice at this point." Leo pauses for a moment, something sinister dancing in his irises. "You know, you don't have to be humble, Aspen. Don't ever be embarrassed of sharing something like that with someone."

"And this is coming from someone who wants to be a surgeon?" I throw back at him, the playfulness in my tone. "The cockiness kind of fits into the stereotypical surgeon mentality."

A ghost of a smile plays on Leo's lips. "Not cocky, love. I'm just pretty fucking confident. If I can't have that image of myself, how do I expect anyone else to feel that way when I need them to trust me with their lives in my hands?"

I stare back at Leo for a moment, mulling over his words. He seemed nice enough, with an arrogance about him, but perhaps I read it in the wrong light. His cockiness wasn't from a place of thinking that he's better than anyone. He has a point. He has to be confident if he wants to thrive in a position like what he's aiming for.

"Am I interrupting something?" Cameron's voice comes from behind me, the sound sliding across my eardrums like silk. There's a coldness in his tone, laced with curiosity.

Whipping my head around, I lift my gaze to his and he raises an eyebrow, keeping his eyes trained on me instead of even bothering to acknowledge Leo.

"Cam," I breathe, rising to my feet as my heart picks up the pace, rattling against my rib cage. "You're here."

"You called and I came, baby," he reminds me, the coldness still lingering in his tone. "Who's your friend?"

Swallowing hard over the knives in my throat, I feel a wave of nausea rolling in the pit of my stomach. "This is Leo. Delilah knows him from the hospital."

"Hmm," Cam murmurs, directing his intense green eyes to Leo. "You can leave now."

Leo snorts as he rises to his feet. "And who the fuck are you?"

"The only one that Aspen will be going home with." Cam's gaze is cold and he doesn't tear his eyes away from Leo as he stares him down. The possessiveness rolls off him in waves and I don't miss the way he tightens his jaw as he challenges Leo to try and take what is his.

"I'm sorry, I didn't realize that Aspen was a piece of property that you needed to come and piss on." Leo narrows his eyes, not backing down from Cam before he glances at me. "Good luck with everything," he tells me, a sadness lingering in his voice. "Maybe I'll see you around Drezel sometime."

Swallowing hard, I offer him a small smile and nod. Glancing at Cam, I stare at the side of his face as he watches Leo walk away. And I can't help but feel like shit for it. I didn't want to pursue anything with Leo, but he seemed nice enough. He didn't do anything wrong that warranted Cam's attitude.

"What the hell, Cameron?" I snap at him as he turns his head to stare at me. "That was completely unnecessary."

He tilts his head to the side, raising an eyebrow at me. "Oh, was it?" Turning his body to face me, the anger vibrates from him, the tension thick in the air. His movements are slow as he walks around the couch, stopping as his toes meet mine. "And how would you feel if the situation were reversed? What if I called you to come to me and you found me with another girl."

"That's not even fair. I swear that it's not what it looks like. We were literally just talking."

Cam's jaw tics. "That's how it always starts, isn't it? A friendly little exchange between two strangers until it grows into something more."

"Do you hear yourself right now?" Rolling my eyes, I throw my hands up in defeat. This is a side of Cameron I haven't seen before. And while his possessiveness may have been hot at first, I have no energy to deal with this shit. "Forget that I called you. You can go home or do whatever the hell it was you were going to do."

As I spin on my heel and begin to walk away from him, his arm darts out, wrapping his hand around my wrist as he hauls me back to him. The front of my body collides with his, but it doesn't throw him off-balance at all. He links his arms around the back of my waist as he holds me close to him.

Tilting my head back, I look up at him and find a fire burning in his gaze as he stares down at me.

"You want to know what it was that I was going to do tonight?" he murmurs, his voice soft as he stares through me. "I was going to come here and pick you up and take you home with me for the night."

My breath catches in my throat, a fire burning in the pit of my stomach as I swallow roughly. Cam lifts the bottom hem of my shirt high enough to slip his fingertips underneath. His palms are warm and soft against my skin, his fingers digging into my flesh as he holds me tighter.

"I guess I didn't make myself clear when I agreed to your little deal." He pauses for a moment, a ghost of a smile playing on his lips. "I'm the only friend that you have benefits with. That's my only condition. We don't have to be in a relationship, but when it comes to fucking around, we're exclusive. I have no intentions of fucking around with anyone else and I expect the same courtesy from you too."

His words shake me straight to my core as it hits me. He felt threatened by Leo because we were together. I know how it probably looked to him, but that wasn't the case at all. It's not worth arguing, since it seems like Cam has already moved on from that and is now making himself crystal clear.

I think about how he must have felt and if roles would have been reversed like he said. He's not asking me for a relationship or anything definitive. Just a mutual respect. If we're friends with benefits, that means no one else. Not that there is anyone else that I would even want.

"You're the only one," I tell him, my voice low as I lift my arms and lace them around the back of his neck. "As long as this is going on between us, there's no one else."

"Good girl," he murmurs, his face dropping down to mine. He nips at my bottom lip, pulling it in between his teeth before he bites down lightly. "Now, can I continue with my plan and take you home?"

Pulling back from him, I slowly lick my lips, the corners of them tugging upward.

"I dare you."

CHAPTER SEVENTEEN
CAMERON

oving my hands from Aspen's waist, I slide my hand into hers and lead her through the house. She picks up the pace, her feet moving quickly to keep up with me as we push through the crowded rooms. I spot Hayden standing over in the corner talking to some girl, and I pause for a moment. Aspen all but runs into my back as I abruptly stop.

She doesn't say a word as I head over to Hayden. His gaze meets mine over the top of the blonde's head in front of him. Eyebrows pulled together, he looks at me cautiously, but his face softens as he sees Aspen with me. Realization dawns on his face and he nods.

"I'll be good," he tells me before I even get a

chance to say anything to him. Hayden rode along with me here, mainly because I asked him to, but he was never someone to turn down a good time. And it looks like he found his good time for the night.

"Are you sure?" I ask him, my voice loud over the bass that vibrates through the speakers throughout the room. "I don't wanna just leave you here alone."

"I'm not alone," he smirks, glancing down at the girl still facing him. "Seriously. Don't worry about me. I'll either get an Uber or find somewhere to stay for the night."

Nodding, I leave Hayden as he directs his attention back to the girl that he found to occupy his time. We've all been there and even though most people know me as the playboy, they hadn't seen anything until Hayden King arrived. That guy runs through girls faster than some people change their underwear. But it's not my place to judge him at all.

Aspen follows along behind me as we step out into the cold air of the night. My car is parked along the curb so it isn't a long walk. She smiles up at me, thanking me as I hold her door open for her and wait for her to get in like a perfect fucking gentleman.

I may not have the best track record when it comes to women, but I know how to be respectful.

Sliding behind the steering wheel, I drop my hand onto Aspen's thigh after I start the engine of my car. She glances over at me, the flames dancing in her irises as she stares me down. So help me God, if she keeps looking at me like that, I'll fuck her right here in the back seat of my car without a second fucking thought.

"You gotta stop looking at me like that if you want to make it back to my place," I warn her, my voice hoarse as my cock strains against my pants.

A smirk plays on her lips and she raises an eyebrow at me. "What if I told you that I didn't want to wait until we got back to your place?" she challenges me, the temptation mixing with the tension in the air between us.

"I'd fuck you in the back seat quick and then take you home and give you a proper fucking in my bed, like the gentleman I am."

Aspen laughs lightly, her face innocent and carefree as she tips her head back slightly. It takes everything in me to tear my eyes away from her and direct my gaze back through the windshield. I swear, I could stare at her for the rest of my life. And I think I just heard my new favorite sound.

"Okay, okay," she resigns as I pull the car away

from the curb and head down the street. "Take me to your bed."

Swallowing roughly, I nod as my cock pulsates in my pants. Tightening my grip on her thigh, my fingertips dig into her flesh and I hold on to her as we cruise down the street. Aspen falls silent, humming along to the music that plays through the speakers as I force myself to keep my eyes off her.

It feels like it takes forever to get back to the house, but we're there before I know it. I pull into my spot, next to Asher's car, and put it in park before killing the engine. Aspen looks over at the two other vehicles and the house before looking back at me.

"You have roommates?"

I nod as I turn to look at her. "Greyson and Asher. Knowing the two of them, they're both probably passed out already." I pause for a moment, tilting my head to the side. "Is that going to be a problem, that I don't live alone?"

Aspen shakes her head, her throat moving as she swallows. "I just wasn't sure how you wanted this arrangement to work out. If you wanted this to be a secret too or not."

"I don't fucking care what anyone sees or thinks," I admit, my voice harsher than intended.

"Let them think what they want. None of that matters to me because they're not the ones involved in this."

"I thought you wanted me to be a secret entirely," she practically whispers as I reach for the door handle. I freeze with the door half open, turning back to look at her.

"You're not a secret. I just don't want anyone to know that I need a fucking tutor," I tell her, the words coming out in a rush. "Trust me, baby. They all already know about you. They just don't know about you helping me with my grades and shit."

I watch her as she visibly relaxes, almost like she can take a deep breath. Her chest rises as she sucks in a breath, her eyes searching mine as she nods. Words fail her as she reaches for her door handle and follows suit, opening her door after I do. Climbing out of the car, I slam the door shut behind me before I go over to her.

Standing by the door, I watch her as she stands upright, her head tilting back to look at me. Her lips part slightly and I push her door shut as I close the distance between us. Aspen lifts her arms, her wrists locking behind my neck as I back her up against the side of the car. My hands are on her hips, my fingers digging into her skin.

"You'll never be a secret, babe," I assure her, my face dipping down to hers. My tongue darts out and I trace the outline of her plump lips before nipping at her bottom lip. "Even if I can't give you my heart, I can at least make sure you're never kept in the dark. You outshine everyone else on this planet and I want to make sure they all fucking know that."

She inhales sharply, her lips parting slightly as my mouth collides with hers. Pressing my body flush against her, I grind my erection against her stomach, feeling the warmth spreading throughout my body from the lust that's been building between the two of us. Aspen moans and I swallow her sounds as she tightens her arms around the back of my neck.

Sliding my hands down to her ass, I lift her into the air and into my arms as she instinctively wraps her legs around my waist. If I don't get her inside right now, I'm going to end up fucking her out here in the parking lot where everyone can see us.

We don't make it past the front of the car as I lay her down on the hood, her legs still locked around me. Feeling the warmth from between the center of her thighs, my cock throbs in protest, wanting to be balls deep inside her. Her lips collide with my mouth, her tongue sliding across mine as they tangle together.

"I can't fuck you here," I whisper against her lips, my voice hoarse and strained with lust. "I'm taking you inside now."

"Take me wherever you want, Cam," she breathes, a moan slipping from her lips as I lift her back into my arms. Her face drops down to my neck as she drags the tip of her tongue along my flesh. "I'm yours to do whatever you please with."

"Trust me, baby... I'm going to make you forget every guy who's been inside you before me."

My hands grip her ass as I carry her inside, not giving a fuck if anyone hears us as I slam the front door shut behind us. My footsteps are heavy as I carry her up the stairs and to my bedroom.

And now I have her right where she belongs...

CHAPTER EIGHTEEN
ASPEN

Cameron carries me into his bedroom, kicking the door shut behind us. It slams, the sound echoing throughout the house, but Cam doesn't seem too concerned with waking up his roommates. He strides across the room before gently laying me down on his bed. My chest rises and falls in rapid succession, my heart pounding erratically in my chest as I stare up at him.

He stares down at me, flames of lust licking at his green irises as he reaches behind his head. Grabbing the collar of his shirt, he pulls it over his tousled hair and drops it onto the floor beside him. He stands in place, allowing my eyes a moment to explore the planes of his torso. My gaze moves across his abs, tracing the dips and curves of his body as I scan his chest, making my way back to his face.

"Your turn, baby," he demands in a husky voice, nodding his head at me. "Either you can take it off or I will."

Biting down on my bottom lip, my teeth leave half-moon indents in my flesh as my eyes search his. A warmth spreads through the pit of my stomach and I clamp my thighs together, looking for any type of friction. "Why don't you come over here and do it for me?"

His throat bobs as he swallows hard, pinning me with his gaze as he begins to stalk closer. As he reaches the bottom of the bed, his hands dart out, grabbing my ankles. I yelp out in surprise as he tugs on me, yanking me toward him. In one swift movement, he pulls me across the bed, until my legs are hanging off the end of it.

Cam releases my ankles, sliding off my shoes and socks before he drags his fingertips up my thighs. As he reaches the bottom hem of my shirt, he slips his hands underneath, stroking my skin underneath the cotton material. His hands reach my shoulders, simultaneously pushing up the fabric as he pulls me into a seated position.

His hands are soft, warming my skin as he pulls

my shirt free from my body. The cool air of the room replaces his touch and a shiver slides down my spine. Cam's palm feels like silk as it moves across my cheek. Wrapping his long fingers around the back of my neck, he tilts my head back as he leans down closer to me, his lips instantly finding mine.

Our mouths collide together, working in tandem as we both taste and tease one another. His lips are soft against mine and he tastes like a hint of mint. He slides his tongue along the seam of my lips, slowly parting them as he dives inside. I let him in, exposing him to the darkest parts of myself as he breathes me in.

Reaching around my back, Cam's hands find the clasp of my bra and he slides them through the hooks. Hooking his fingers under the straps, he slides them from my shoulders and down my arms until my breasts are free from the fabric.

He moves away from me for a moment, pulling back as his eyes scan my body. I swallow hard under his gaze, watching the way his gaze trails over my breasts as he discards my bra on the floor with the rest of our clothes. Cam crouches down in front of me, trailing his fingertips along my collarbones before making his way down my torso.

A soft moan slips from my lips as Cam slides one

of his palms underneath my breast, taking it in his hand as he kneads my flesh. Planting his other palm against my collarbone, he rises to his feet as he pushes me back onto the bed. Following along with me, he parts my legs with his knee as he climbs over me. Settling between my thighs, he props himself up so I don't take all of his weight as he brings his mouth down to my nipple.

His tongue swirls around my flesh as he slowly draws it in between his teeth. He sucks and bites, tasting and teasing my skin as he rolls my other nipple with the tips of his fingers. I'm a mess under his touch, writhing on the bed as he explores my body, finding what makes me tick. My nails dig into his back, marking his skin with scratches as I tilt my head, getting lost in what his mouth feels like on me.

"Fuck, Aspen," he breathes, his voice hoarse and strained as he lifts his head. His eyes meet mine as he presses his lips to the skin between both of my breasts. "You're driving me fucking crazy."

He drags his tongue along my skin, moving down my body. Nipping and sucking my skin as he makes his way toward my waist, he slides his fingers under the waistband of my pants. Curling his fingers, he hooks them in the fabric and slowly begins to peel my pants and my underwear from my body in one fluid movement.

Lifting my hips, I move my ass from the bed as he pushes my clothes down my thighs. He moves off the bed, rising to his feet again as he pulls my pants and underwear past my feet and tosses them onto the ground. I'm completely naked under his gaze and I can feel him staring through me, like he's staring into the fibers of my soul.

"Jesus Christ," he groans, running his hand through his dark hair. His throat bobs as he swallows hard, a wave of pain passing through his eyes as he drinks me in. It's contradictory, but I don't question him on it as the flames of desire wash it away.

Cameron undoes his pants, shoving them down his thighs in a haste. His boxers slide down with the soft material, his cock hard as a rock as he frees it from his clothing. I swallow hard, gulping as my eyes take in this length. Not only is he packing... but it's fucking thick too.

"What's wrong, baby girl?" he murmurs, as he climbs over me and settles between my legs. Completely ignoring his erection, he strokes the sides of my face, concern laced in his eyes.

A ragged breath slips from my lips as I search his

green eyes. "I don't know that it's going to fit," I whisper, that panic filling me as I'm overcome with thoughts of him stretching me beyond belief. I literally don't know that it's physically possible.

"I promise I won't hurt you, Aspen," he breathes, dragging his fingertips down the length of my throat. "If you don't want to do this, we don't have to."

I shake my head, biting down on my bottom lip. Cam frowns, his mouth finding mine as he pulls my lip from my teeth with his own. His tongue darts out, licking the indents that I felt in my flesh. "I want you. I want this."

"Do you trust me?" he asks, his voice soft as his eyes desperately search mine. There's something lingering in his expression, something that resembles fear. I don't think that he's afraid to hurt me, but he's frightened of what my answer might possibly be.

And there's no reason for his fear, because he's never given me a reason not to trust him.

"Yes," I breathe, nodding as I assure him that this is what I want with him. "I trust you, Cameron."

I watch his expression transform, a ragged breath of relief slipping from his lips before his mouth collides with mine again. He steals the air from my lungs, draining all of the oxygen from my body as my head swims in pure ecstasy from the taste of him as his tongue slides against mine.

Cam breaks apart for a moment, reaching over to his nightstand as he pulls out a condom. Grabbing the wrapper between his teeth, he tears it open before sliding the condom over his hard cock. I watch in awe as he positions himself against me. There's no need for any lube because I'm already soaked, practically panting with the need to feel him inside me.

"Look at me, baby," he murmurs, his eyes searching mine as I lift my gaze to his. "I got you."

His lips are soft against mine as he distracts me while sliding inside me. There's no resistance, although he stretches me wide open as he fills me to the brim in one thrust. Surprisingly, there's no pain and only pleasure. I've never experienced someone quite as large as him, so it was intimidating.

But now with him inside me, it feels like this is where he's always belonged.

"See," he says, his voice low as a smirk plays on his lips. "I told you that I got you. It feels like I fit inside you perfectly."

"Mmm," I moan in response as he shifts his hips,

slowly thrusting into me before he pauses. "Don't stop."

Cam gives me a heated stare, the smile falling from his lips as he slides his hand down under my ass, lifting my hips to get a better angle. "Oh, I'm just getting started, babe."

My nails dig into his back and I scratch at his skin as we climb higher together. With one hand gripping my ass, the other slides up along my throat as he pounds into me. He grabs my chin, jerking my head toward him as his lips collide with mine once again.

Moaning into his mouth, I move my hips against him, fighting for the friction I feel against my clit as his hips dig into me. He thrusts harder, his cock filling me with every movement. His hand leaves my face, the other abandoning my ass as he grabs my hips. Cam pulls away from me, lifting up to his knees. He slowly pulls out of me, cold air meeting my skin as I instantly feel his absence.

A frown forms on my lips, my eyebrows tugging together as I stare up at him in confusion. He gives me a heated stare, a smirk playing on his lips as he grips my hips tighter and flips me onto my stomach. The air leaves my lungs in a whoosh, a yelp falling from my lips as he moves me effortlessly. He doesn't loosen his grip as he pulls me onto my knees with my ass in the air.

Cam positions himself behind me and slowly thrusts back into me. With this angle, he fills me even deeper than before and I don't bother swallowing back the moan before it escapes me. His one hand is gripping my ass, as he slides the other along my spine, pressing my chest against the bed. Abandoning my ass, he slides his fingers along my skin, moving to the front of my body and only stopping as they brush against my clit.

"Fuck, baby," he moans, rocking into me again, his fingers pressing against my clit as he rolls them over the small bundle of nerves. "I want to feel you coming all over my cock."

I see fucking stars as he shifts his hips, slamming back into me. It feels like he's in my rib cage and I moan against the mattress as I turn my head to the side. "Then don't stop," I breathe, my voice hoarse as he plays with my clit, thrusting his cock back into me.

"Didn't plan on it," he groans, his fingers working over me. He has me in his hands, playing me like a skilled musician. It isn't long before I'm climbing higher and higher, closer to the edge. As I reach the top of the cliff, Cam slams into me again, successfully shoving me over the edge.

I'm falling into the abyss of ecstasy as my body shatters around him. The warmth consumes me and my orgasm tears through my body like a fucking earthquake. Cameron isn't far behind me, moaning my name with his release as he rocks his hips against me once more. His movements are slowing and my legs are quaking as he pulls his hand away from my clit.

My head swims, the euphoria almost too much for me to handle as I collapse onto the bed. Cam rises to his feet, pulling the condom from his cock before tossing it over into the small trash can beside his nightstand. Cam disappears for a moment as I settle on his bed, my chest rising and falling in rapid succession with each shallow breath.

He isn't gone for long, reappearing as he slips into the room with a warm washcloth for me. He softly closes the door behind him, as if we haven't already woken up the entire house with how loud we were being. Rolling onto my side, I take the washcloth from him as he presses it between my thighs. Cam's eyes meet mine, his gaze unreadable as he lies down on the bed next to me.

"That was an experience," I tell him, my lips curling upward as a soft chuckle escapes me.

Cam cocks an eyebrow and flashes his bright white teeth at me as he closes the space between us on the bed. His lips brush against mine before his deep green eyes meet my paler ones. "Baby, baby, baby," he murmurs, dragging his fingertips down the side of my torso. "That was just the beginning. We're nowhere close to being done..."

CHAPTER NINETEEN
CAMERON

Leaving my advisor's office, I feel like a weight has been lifted off my shoulders. My grades have been rising and I've officially gotten my biology grade exactly where I need it to be to maintain my scholarship. Coach will be pleased because now I no longer need to worry about potentially losing game time. It was my biggest fear and it seriously feels like I can breathe now without feeling the weight of it all.

I owe it all to Aspen. There's no way I would have been able to do it without her. And thankfully, even though my grade is up, she's still agreed to help me the rest of the semester. God knows, if I let her get away now, I'm bound to end up failing and losing it all.

Aspen is already waiting for me in the library when I get there. In typical fashion, she has her notes and books spread out on the table. A smile touches my lips as I watch her from afar for a moment, admiring her beauty.

We haven't really spoken since I dropped her off yesterday morning. And it wasn't awkward between us when I gave her a ride back to her apartment. After the night that we had together, I can only imagine that she needed to rest, because I was fucking exhausted afterward.

It's weird... this friends with benefits thing. Even though Saturday night was our first time truly crossing into the benefits area, I haven't been able to get her out of my head. And that's not the way this arrangement is supposed to play out. No strings attached, and that includes the ones my brain is trying to fucking create.

Aspen has definitely worked her way under my skin and I'm not so sure that I like it. It feels too comfortable, like that's exactly where she belongs, and I don't want her to. But I don't want her anywhere else... I don't want her anywhere but with me.

As I walk over to the table, Aspen lifts her gaze from her notes in front of her, her eyes meeting mine as a soft smile touches her lips. "Hey," she says quietly, her irises glimmer under the lights above.

"Hey you," I murmur, fighting the urge to capture her plump lips with my own.

Chill the fuck out, Cam.

"Sorry that I was a few minutes late," I tell her, glancing at my watch again before taking the seat next to her. "My meeting with my advisor ran over and I had to shower after practice so I didn't come here smelling like disgusting hockey equipment."

Aspen laughs lightly, turning her head to look at me. "Well, if it makes you feel any better, my senses do not detect any gross smells."

A smirk forms on my lips as I lean back and place my arm across the back of her chair. "So, you're saying I smell good then?"

She tilts her head to the side. "I didn't say that. I've smelled the smell in your car when your bag is in there. You smell better than that, but that's as far as I'm going with feeding your ego right now."

"Ah, baby," I chuckle softly, the term of endearment slipping out before I can stop it. It doesn't even fucking matter anymore. I can call her whatever the hell I want. Even though we're not together, she's still mine. "You keep me humble."

"Someone has to," she quips, winking at me as

she picks up her pen and taps it on her notebook in front of her. "Now, you need to focus so we can go through this shit for tomorrow's exam."

A ghost of a smile plays on my lips as I scan her face, free from any makeup. She's naturally beautiful and I can feel it in my core. Fuck, she isn't just under my skin. She's the marrow inside my goddamn bones. "It's hard to focus sitting this close to you."

"There's a chair on the opposite side of the table."

Shaking my head at her, I can't fight the smirk that forms. She keeps me on my toes with her quick responses and I love it. "That chair is reserved for the friend zone. Sitting next to you comes as another added benefit to our friendship."

Aspen rolls her eyes at me, but I don't miss the grin she attempts to bite back as a pink tint spreads across her cheeks. "How did your meeting go with your advisor?"

"You're never going to believe this," I start, unable to contain the excitement in my voice. "We did it. My biology grade is officially where it needs to be. My scholarship is safe and so is my place on the team."

I watch as her eyes widen, her smile spreading across her entire fucking face as she stares at me with so much pride. "That's amazing, Cam! Seriously, I'm so proud of you. I knew you would be able to do it."

"I wouldn't have been able to do it without you," I admit, my voice hoarse as my eyes bounce back and forth between hers. "Seriously, Aspen. You're my saving grace. I literally owe you everything."

"Nonsense," she shakes her head, a wave of shyness passing through her. She's discrediting and dismissing everything she's done to get me to this point. "You don't owe me anything. Just make sure your grade doesn't slip again."

My eyebrows tug together for a moment. "Are you saying you're done with me now? I thought we had an agreement, that you would help me through the rest of the semester?"

Aspen tilts her head to the side. "Do you still want me to? I'm not saying I don't want to, because if I can help you, I most definitely want to. But are you sure you still need me?"

More than you'll ever fucking know...

"Yes." The word comes out in a rush and I don't even care how desperate it sounds. "I don't think I can do it without you."

Her lips curl upward. "Then I'm not going anywhere," she breathes, a fire burning in her eyes as the flames lick at her irises. She clears her throat, collecting herself as she turns her gaze back to the notes in front of her. "We'd better get to studying then because you have to pass the exam tomorrow."

"Yes, ma'am," I chuckle, attempting to lighten the mood.

No strings, just a friends with benefits arrangement. Saturday was nothing more or nothing less than that. Just two friends indulging in our benefits.

For some reason, it feels like there's something different between us now. Like there's been a shift, and I can't quite put my finger on it. And the way she's burrowed herself into my bones, I'm not sure I want to even acknowledge it at this point—let alone discuss it.

And this is when I just let it ride and see where this goes.

Which is hopefully not up in fucking flames...

CHAPTER TWENTY
ASPEN

We go through the rest of the material that is going to be covered on the exam tomorrow and it doesn't take long for Cameron to show that he really doesn't need me. Our intense tutoring and study sessions lately have proven a lot in terms of his mental capabilities. He almost played it off like he was stupid, but he's not in the slightest.

He has a different style of learning and once I was able to figure that out, it was easy to teach him the material. I could easily pass him my notes after class and he would know enough from that. We could completely bypass these sessions altogether.

I'm not saying that that's what I want. Because once this arrangement is over, I think our other one goes along with it. And we're only getting started with the added benefits to our friendship.

Saturday night was an experience with him I don't think I will ever be able to erase from my mind. And I'm not sure I ever want to. Even if this is all our friendship will ever be—even if it ends after this semester—there is an undeniable connection between us and it's evident after what happened between us the other night.

Cameron Sawyer is unlike anyone I've ever met... and I'm not sure I'm ready to let him go after the end of the semester. And I'm not sure what scares me more—the thought of the semester ending and this being done between us or the fact that I'm not ready for this to end.

Feelings aren't an option and I need all of these feelings to disappear immediately.

"So, are you doing anything this weekend?" Cam asks me as he helps me close up my books and tucks them into my bag for me. "I know Delilah likes to attempt to drag you out to parties, even though that's not your scene."

I cringe as the memory of the party Delilah took me to this past Saturday plays on repeat in my mind. I should really track down Leo and apologize for the way Cam behaved. I would be lying if I said it didn't turn me on, but I felt kind of bad. And plus, if I end up going to med school at Drezel, Leo could prove to be a valuable resource there.

"Yeah, no," I shake my head, a nervous laugh falling from my lips. "Next time she drags me to a party, it's not going to be one where there's a bunch of random people. You're right, it's not my scene."

Cam's lips curl upward as he slowly stands up, grabbing the strap of my bag as he throws it over his shoulder. I swear my heart melts a little and I need an ice rink to get that shit back into solid form. "I know hockey games might not be your scene either, but I was wondering if you wanted to come to my game? I have one Saturday night and I know that we talked about you coming sometime..."

He shifts his weight nervously and for the first time, his confidence is hanging in the balance. Usually, he's arrogant and comes off as cocky because he's so sure of himself, which isn't a bad thing. But as he stands here, his eyes searching mine, I can't help but feel like he's let his guard down and he doesn't know how to handle the possibility of my rejection.

Tilting my head to the side, a smile touches my lips. "I would love to. I wasn't sure when your next one was and didn't want to sound weird asking to come, even though we talked about it before."

Cam visibly relaxes, his chest heaving as he lets out the breath he was holding. His expression softens, and where is that damn freezer I need to shove my melting heart back into?

"Babe. I want you at every single one of my games if you want to go," he says softly, reaching out as he brushes a piece of hair away from my face and tucks it behind my ear. His fingertips are soft as they linger along my skin, slowly sliding them down the length of my throat. "Seriously. The thought of you sitting there watching me does something that I don't even know how to put into words."

And that's it. I'm practically a puddle on the floor around his damn feet.

"I mean, I've never been to a game before so I'm not sure I'll fully understand what is going on, but I would love to be there to support you," I whisper, not fully trusting my voice as he already has my insides feeling like mush. "Honestly, I think it would be pretty cool to see you in action. Especially when I know how important it is to you. It's your passion and I appreciate you wanting to share that side of you with me."

His face softens, his expression unreadable as I

feel him staring directly into my soul. The look on his face rocks me to my core. His lips part slightly, but no words come out as he continues to stare at me for a moment. "I'll tell Isla that you'll be coming too. Do you care if I give her your number? That way you can find her and she can show you to your seats and everything."

"That would be perfect," I tell him, feeling a sense of relief. I don't know Isla very well, but she's his best friend's girlfriend and his other best friend's sister. I'm not sure how that whole thing worked out between the three of them, but more power to them.

I've seen Logan and Isla in the halls together and if you ask me, they seem like the ultimate power couple. I've heard through the grapevine about their struggles when their secret came out about their relationship and how her brother, August, didn't handle it too well. Actually, I was at the party with Delilah the night he found out.

I had happened to step outside for a breath of fresh air when I saw the entire encounter go down. It's something I never bothered to speak to anyone about because it was none of my business. But it seems like they had worked out their differences and things were good now.

According to Cam, August has his own shit that he's dealing with now. He's been trying to work things out with a girl he got pregnant. I don't know the specifics of their relationship, but from what I've overheard, it seems like it comes down to what it always does with these guys...

Hockey is always the most important thing in their lives and it seems like August is struggling to balance between that and having a baby coming into the world soon.

But then again, who am I to judge? I don't really know any of them, but I just know what I've heard through Cam and other people. Everyone has their own shit they're working through and it's only right that I mind my own business. All I can do is hope for the best for everyone. Kindness is fucking free and isn't handed out as often as it should be.

"You still with me, Rossi?" Cameron breaks into my rambling thoughts. I quickly look back at him, his face coming back into focus. It's a problem I struggle with, mainly from my ADHD and the fact that my meds are probably wearing off this late in the evening.

"Yeah, sorry about that," I smile sheepishly and shrug as I attempt to brush it off dismissively.

Cameron's eyebrows draw together and he tilts

his head to the side. "You don't have to apologize, but where did you go, babe?"

Swallowing hard, I turn on my heel, heading toward the door as it feels like the walls of the library are beginning to close in on me. I can feel Cam hot on my heels as he follows me out into the hall. I pick up my pace, heading straight through the doors that lead outside, and inhale the cold air.

Cameron has his little secret about his grades and being tutored, but he doesn't know about my secret that I don't let anyone know about.

His arm darts out, his hand wrapping around my shoulder as he pulls me to a halt. Both of his hands grip me and he spins me around to face him. Tilting my head back, I meet his gaze as his eyes desperately search mine. "Don't ever run from me, baby," he whispers, his voice cracking over his words. "You drifted away. I get it, it happens to people. I didn't mean to run you off by prying. I was just wondering where you went."

I swallow hard over the knives in my throat. I didn't really want to share my secret with him because when people know is when they begin to judge. Over the years, I learned how to act appropriately around people, and therapy and my meds were a big part of that. Considering the fact that my GPA is impeccable, I don't want people knowing that I take ADHD medications.

Most college students take them to help them study to try and get better grades. I take them because I need them. Because I can't focus or complete normal tasks without them. The last thing I need is for people to think that my success in my studies comes just from taking my medication as prescribed.

"You know how this little tutoring arrangement is your secret?" My nostrils flare as I inhale deeply. "If I tell you my secret, can you keep it too?"

Cameron stares directly through me, as if he's looking into a mirror through my eyes. "Your secrets are always safe with me, Aspen."

I swallow hard, second-guessing myself before I let him in. "I was diagnosed with ADHD in high school. I take medication every day and it usually wears off around this time, which can cause me to dissociate without even realizing it. Sometimes I just drift off without trying and focus on listening." I pause for a moment, my eyes searching his with desperation. "No one can know, though. I don't want people thinking that I have the grades that I do just from taking medications."

His lips part slightly, his eyebrows drawn

together almost as if he's going to argue with me. Instead, I watch his throat bob as he swallows and nods. "I'll take your secret to the grave with me," he whispers, stepping into my space as he slides his palm to cup the side of my face. His face drops down to mine. "But none of that defines you, baby. You're amazing and fucking brilliant with or without meds. And you never have to feel like you need to hide any of that from me."

And just like that, Cameron fucking Sawyer rips open my rib cage and crawls inside, making his home in my heart.

And I'll never forgive him for it.

CHAPTER TWENTY-ONE
CAMERON

"So, I heard that Aspen was supposed to be meeting Isla here tonight to watch the game," Logan says as he sits down on the bench beside me. He's already suited and ready to hit the ice. Bending forward, I start to lace my skates, tightening them as I make my way toward the top.

Not looking in his direction, I begin to tie them. "Yeah. I invited her to come watch and figured since your girlfriend never misses a game, she could show her where the seats are and everything."

Logan is silent for a moment as I finish tying my skates. As I sit upright and glance over at him, I notice his gaze already trained on me. "It's just different. You've never invited a girl to any of our games before."

His words weigh heavily in my mind and I know how it might look to him. He's right, this is the first time I've ever had a girl sitting in the stands watching me. And thinking about that makes me feel unsettled. It's out of character for me, given my playboy status, but I can't read into it like he is.

I refuse to... because if I read into it then that means it might be more than it actually is.

"We've been hanging out and shit and she's never been to a game before, so I figured maybe she would want to come see one," I offer, shrugging dismissively as I pull my helmet over my head and snap the straps in place.

"Right," he raises an eyebrow in suspicion as he nods. "So, what's going on between the two of you, exactly? I know you've been hanging out with her and everything. And Hayden told me about you leaving with her at the party."

My jaw clenches. What's going on between us isn't a secret from anyone, I just haven't had this conversation with Logan yet and I don't like the way he's looking at me. Like he knows something I don't. "We're just friends," I tell him, which isn't a lie. "You know, with benefits... but nothing more than that."

A chuckle vibrates in his chest as he rolls his eyes at me. "You've had plenty of friends with benefits before and never have they ended up at one of your games."

"What are you trying to say, Knight?" I bite at him, unable to keep the harshness from my tone.

"Nothing." He shakes his head dismissively. "Just simply making an observation."

"Yo!" Hayden calls over to us as he stands with August by the door. "What are the two of you doing? We gotta get out there before Coach gets pissed."

"We're coming," Logan answers him as he rises to his feet and glances back at me. "I wasn't meaning to pry, Cam," he tells me, his voice apologetic. "Sometimes it just feels like we're growing apart and I want you to know you can talk to me about shit."

Standing up with him, I grab my gloves and stick and nod. "I know, bro. My bad for being MIA lately. I know I can talk to you and if I ever need to, I will. I'm telling you, we're just friends, though. You know me. Even with the benefits, it won't go any further than that."

"You're right," he laughs lightly as we both begin to stroll toward the other guys and follow them down the tunnel. "Isla was pretty excited to hang out with her since she knows the two of you have been hanging out. She'll be in good hands with her."

"I know she will," I say, smiling at him. "Your girl's a good one."

"Damn straight," he agrees, grinning like a love-struck fool. "And that's why I'm not ever going to let her go. Trust me, one day, you'll find someone who will change your mind about your thoughts on attachments. And when you find her, you better hold on to her for dear fucking life."

Hayden glances back at us as we reach the ice, rolling his eyes. "Can you two girls quit with the sappy shit and get your heads out of your asses? We have a game to win."

Logan gives him the middle finger before sliding his hands into his gloves. A laugh falls from my lips as I slide my mouth guard over my teeth and I slip my hands into my gloves. We all rush out onto the ice and begin our warm-ups before the game starts.

As I skate past the boards, I glance up at the stands and see Aspen sitting there, bundled up in a winter coat with a beanie pulled over her head. She's sitting beside Isla, smiling as her eyes meet mine from up above. Lifting my hand, I wave to her and she gives me a small one back. Logan's words drift into my mind and I push them away as I skate back toward the other guys for warm-ups.

It isn't long before the ref blows the whistle and it's time to get ready for the puck drop. Everyone lines up in their respective places and August takes the center as he faces off with the center from the other team. They both lower themselves closer to the ice, their sticks in position as the ref drops the puck onto the ice.

The other team wins the face-off and they get the puck first. They pass it back and forth, making their way down the ice toward our defensive zone. Hayden and Logan are both there, waiting and anticipating their moves. It isn't long before we take possession of the puck and we're skating back in the opposite direction.

August is out in the center, stickhandling the puck as he skates toward the net, when one of their defensemen checks him and the puck gets away from him. They take the puck around the back of the net, attempting to send it around the boards and back to center ice when I intercept the shot.

Driving my shoulder into one of the other team's defensemen, I slam him into the boards in a clean hit as I steal the puck from him. August is skating toward the center and I see Simon over to the right side of the net. August has someone guarding him and I don't have a clear pass to him. Skating toward the center, I get into a better position to send it sailing across to Simon.

Simon gets the puck before the guy who is supposed to be on him does. August manages to break free from his opponent. I watch as Simon passes it to him, clearly getting an assist as August sends the puck barreling past the goalie and into the net. The horn sounds and everyone celebrates, yelling out as we score our first goal.

Playing with these guys is literally a dream fucking come true. The end goal is making it professionally, but we are literally the dream team. The way we all work together like a well-oiled machine is a force to be reckoned with. Which is exactly why we're sitting first place in the league right now.

It's shift change and I skate back over to the bench, hopping the boards as I glance up at the stands. Aspen looks like she's sitting on the edge of her seat, fully immersed in the game, and it makes my heart soar. Her gaze meets mine, her cheeks flushed and a smile forms on her lips.

This fucking girl. I thought she could potentially be a distraction sitting in the stands, but there's an overwhelming sense of wanting to make her proud.

Seeing the smile on her face, I know I made the right choice inviting her here. She makes me want to play even better and not just to show off to her.

To make her proud.

To make her fall in love with the sport that has my life in a vise grip.

And if I can help it, I will make sure she doesn't fall in love with me in the process.

———————

It isn't a surprise as the game comes to an end and we leave the ice with another victory. As I make my way to the tunnel, I notice that Isla and Aspen are rising from their seats and following the crowd of people out of the arena. My heart sinks for a moment, but I know she's not going to get too far.

When I get back to my locker, I shove my gloves into my bag and don't bother taking off the rest of my gear as I pull out my phone and open my messages. Just because she came to my game doesn't mean I'm done with her for tonight.

CAMERON

Where are you running off to, baby girl?

Locking my screen, I set my phone down for a moment as I begin to strip out of all of my pads and gear, hastily shoving it all into my bag as I wait for her reply. The guys are all talking, still hyped from our win, but all that I can think about is what Aspen's doing for the rest of the night.

My phone vibrates from the bench, the screen lighting up as I sit down and begin to unlace my skates and slide my feet out of them. Hayden is sitting next to me now and he raises an eyebrow at me as he sees Aspen's name on the screen, but he doesn't say anything.

Usually he's an asshole, but he's surprisingly been the only one who hasn't questioned shit between the two of us. And maybe that's why Hayden King and I were always closer, while August and Logan had the relationship like the two of us do.

ASPEN

> Well, the game was over and it seemed kind of strange to keep sitting in the stands.

CAMERON

> You didn't leave yet, did you?

I set my phone back down for a moment as I put

my skates into my bag and grab a change of clean
clothes from the one part of my bag that doesn't
have disgusting hockey gear in it. It vibrates again
just as I rise to my feet and I quickly unlock the
screen as I go to her message.

ASPEN

> I was walking out to the parking lot
> with Isla. She said she was heading
> home, since Logan and August
> were just going back there. She
> said we could come over there to
> hang out if we wanted to.

Swallowing hard, I reread her message again. As
much as I want them all to get to know her, I want
her to myself tonight.

CAMERON

> Tell her you'll take a rain check. We
> can plan something for next
> weekend, but I had other plans for
> us tonight. I wanted to take
> you out.

ASPEN

> Okay, I'll tell her. Do you want me to
> wait for you here? Or meet you
> somewhere?

A smile touches my lips and I shake my head at her, even though she can't see me.

CAMERON

> I'm getting a quick shower. Wait for me and we'll take my car. We can get yours later.

Or tomorrow...

Locking my phone, I tuck it back in my locker, not needing a response from her. She'll wait for me and I plan on only being in the shower long enough to wash away the stink and sweat from my body. Hayden looks over at me, a ghost of a smirk playing on his lips.

"I'm going to make a wild guess that you already have plans tonight?"

A laugh rumbles in my chest. "You would be right."

"Then I won't even bother inviting you out," he says, laughing with me. "Just be careful with her, bro."

Grabbing my stuff for the shower, I glance over my shoulder at him as I turn to walk away. "I'm always careful."

"You know what I mean," he warns, his voice

low and filled with concern. "You get in too deep and someone's bound to get hurt."

I don't bother responding to him as I head toward the showers, swallowing down the dread that attempts to lodge itself in my throat. I can already feel her dragging me into the depths of her ocean and even though I'm ready to drown myself in her, I can't.

If I stick to my plan, I won't be the one who gets hurt.

But the thought of hurting her doesn't feel any fucking better.

CHAPTER TWENTY-TWO
ASPEN

Sitting in Cameron's car as he drives us from the restaurant, I can't help but close my eyes and deeply inhale his scent. It fills the space between us and he smells amazing, after having just showered before we went out. It definitely beats the smell of sweat and hockey. He's been relatively quiet, like he's been lost in his own thoughts, and the last thing I want to do is overstep any boundaries.

He had surprised me when he texted me after the game, letting me know he already had plans for us. The plans ended up with us going out to eat at a quaint little restaurant in the city. It was a farm-to-table style that I had never been to before. The food was amazing and the conversation between us flowed, just as it always does.

But now that we're driving back, with the night coming to an end, I can't help but feel an overwhelming sense that I'm not ready for this to be over.

As we get close to the ice rink, Cam abruptly pulls his car off onto the side of the street and puts it in park before turning to face me. "I don't want to be too forward and just take you back to my place now, so I need to hear it from you first." He pauses for a moment, wetting his lips with his tongue. "I'm not ready to go our separate ways this evening. Come stay with me for the night?"

Swallowing hard, I get lost in his gaze for a moment before nodding. "Can you drop me off at my car and I'll follow you over? That way you don't have to bring me back tomorrow morning to get it."

He stares at me for a moment before putting the car back in drive. He doesn't bother to argue with me, but I can't help but feel like he wanted me to just go with him and worry about my car tomorrow. Thankfully, Cameron is somewhat of a gentleman— despite his playboy persona—and he's always thoughtful enough to ask me what I want first.

After pulling into the parking lot, he stops his

car in the spot next to mine. He glances back over at me, reaching across the center console as he wraps his hand around the back of my neck and pulls me closer to him. Our lips collide, melting together as his tongue slips into my mouth and tangles with mine. He leaves me breathless, stealing the air from my lungs before abruptly pulling back with a smirk on his lips.

"I'll wait for you, but hurry up," he whispers as he releases the side of my face and settles back into his seat. It takes me a moment to catch my breath and then I'm hopping out of his car and slipping into mine. Wasting no time, I turn on the engine and put it in drive as I follow behind him, pulling out of the parking lot.

Cameron speeds down the street and I struggle to keep up with him as we go faster than the legal speed limit. My heart pounds erratically in my chest, a wild grin on my face as the adrenaline courses through my body. The thought to challenge him and pass him crosses my mind, but I push the dangerous thought away and decide to just follow closely behind him.

It isn't long before we're pulling up to his place and I pull off and park on the side of the road. Cam hops out of his car, heading over to mine as he opens the door for me. As I get out, he slides his hand into mine, lacing our fingers together. Shutting the door behind me, I follow after Cam as he leads me toward the house without a single word.

It's quiet inside when we get there and his stride is long as he leads me to his bedroom. I step into the middle of the room, spinning on my heel to face him as he closes the door and locks it. His eyes lift to mine, his gaze heated as he stalks toward me, closing the distance between us.

His hands find the zipper to my coat, sliding it down before he slides his palms along my shoulders and pushes my jacket from my body. It falls to the floor behind me and the two of us completely ignore it. Cam's palm is warm against the side of my face as he slides his fingers into my hair, pulling me close to him until our mouths crash together.

Lips melting together, bodies flush against one another, I can't stand the anticipation between us right now. After the explosive night that we had together the other night, I need him now. And lord knows that this man can run a fucking marathon, so this will only be round one of the many tonight.

Cam grabs the bottom hem of my shirt, pushing it up my torso until he reaches my neck. Lifting my arms into the air, we break apart but only long enough for him to pull my shirt over my head. Following his lead, I do the same with the material that clings to his body, freeing him until he's naked from the waist up. He reaches behind me, unhooking my bra before peeling it away from me.

Grabbing my hips, he directs me back to the bed, gently pushing me down as he stares at me from where he's standing. "Take off your leggings and your panties," he demands as he undoes his jeans and shoves them down his legs. He takes his boxers with him, freeing his cock as he strips himself of his clothes.

My eyes fall to his erection that stands at full attention, throbbing with how hard it is. Swallowing roughly, I lift my gaze back to his, staring at him as I begin to push my leggings down my legs. Hooking my fingers in the waistband of my thong, I peel that from my body, pulling my feet from them and tossing them onto the floor. I'm completely exposed under his watchful eyes.

"Fuck, Aspen," he groans, licking his lips as he shifts his weight on his feet. "You're so fucking beautiful, spread out on my bed ready for me to fuck you into oblivion."

Raising an eyebrow at him, I spread my legs wider, dragging my finger down my body until I reach my wet pussy. I slide a finger through my folds, teasing him as I stare him down. "So, what are you waiting for?"

"Goddamn," he growls, reaching over to the nightstand as he pulls out a condom. He's vicious with the way he tears it with his teeth and just drops the wrapper onto the floor. I watch him as he rolls it down his length before stalking toward me, climbing on the bed over me. "I'm sorry, baby, but the foreplay will have to come later. Right now, I just need to be inside you, fucking that sweet pussy until you come apart for me."

He settles between my legs, pressing the head of his cock inside me as he slowly slides inside. A moan falls from my lips, my head tilting back against the mattress as he fills me in one fluid movement. Cam grabs one of my thighs, lifting it toward my body as he holds it from behind my knee. My leg is pressed against my chest and he stares down at me.

"Gonna fuck you now, baby," he murmurs, his face dipping down to mine as he bites at my bottom lip. "Gonna fuck you hard."

Sliding my hands through his hair, I grip the back of his head as I hold his face to mine while he begins to move. Our mouths melt together, but there's such an urgency behind it. Our touches are no longer gentle, instead rough. His lips bruise mine, leaving his mark on my body and soul as he pounds into me relentlessly.

He drives me fucking wild, his grip on my thigh tightening as he fucks me harder. I can't take it any longer and I swear that I'm coming apart at the seams, about to explode into a million pieces. I've never felt anything like what I feel with him and I never want this to end.

Pulling away from me, he shifts back onto his shins, lifting my ass in the air as he pulls my thighs up against his chest. Hooking my feet behind his head, he holds me up as he rocks onto his knees and thrusts into me. His hips move quicker and harder. My eyes trail over his body, watching the way his muscles ripple as he takes complete control over my body.

As my eyes meet his again, I'm rocked to my core by the way he's looking at me. His lips are parted slightly, ragged breaths slipping out as he continues to pound into me. He stares down at me with a look I've never seen. A storm brews in his green irises and I don't dare look away from him.

He slams into me again and again until I'm calling out his name, coming apart at the seams. My orgasm tears through my body, my pussy clenching around his cock as he drives me past the point of euphoria. Cam comes with me, his body rocking against me as he thrusts into me once more.

Sweat beads along his hairline and we're both out of breath as he stares down at me. His gaze is heated, his eyes slightly wide as he stares down at me in wonderment.

"Jesus Christ, Aspen," he murmurs breathlessly as he still has my legs in the air and his cock inside me. "What the fuck are you doing to me?"

I stare back up at him, my lips parting slightly as a ragged breath slips from them. Words completely fail me and his question lingers in the air because I'm asking myself the same damn question.

What the fuck are you doing to me, *Cameron?*

CHAPTER TWENTY-THREE
CAMERON

I t's been almost four days since I've last seen Aspen and it's been driving me wild. Since we have our regional championship games coming up soon, Coach has been having us practice almost every day, whether it's on or off the ice. As much as I didn't want to cancel any of my tutoring sessions with Aspen, I had no choice.

Hockey was the driving force behind the tutoring sessions anyway, so it wouldn't make much sense if I would be the one causing myself to lose ice time just so I can see her. I could have made an effort, made some type of an attempt to see her on a different level, but I don't know if I like the way things have been going.

What started out as a simple arrangement is

becoming much more complicated than I would have ever imagined. We had a deal—no feelings involved. So why the fuck can't I get this girl out of my head?

I refuse to admit the real reason, but it lingers in the back of my mind every day. Whenever my thoughts drift to her, I always wonder what she's doing and what she would be doing if she were with me instead. I can't help myself and I know I'm getting in far too deep. Eventually, I'm going to have to cut this shit off and it's only going to be harder to let go the more we get involved with each other.

We had an early practice today, so I had told Aspen that I would still be able to meet her in the evening to go over some of our material from class. To be honest, I'm not sure I even need her help anymore. My grade has by far exceeded my expectations and even if I were to fail a few more exams, I think I would still be okay without her help.

But then that would mean I wouldn't get to see her.

As I pull up to the campus after running home to shower, Aspen sends me a text, asking if I wanted to meet at her apartment instead. It turns out that they were rearranging some of the areas in the library tonight, so it was closed for any studying. Going to her place is the only option and the last thing I'm going to do is say no, even though I should.

Her apartment is a short drive away and it isn't long before I'm pulling into a parking spot and heading inside the building. I hop onto the elevator and take it up to her floor. Pulling out my phone as I walk down the hall, I text her to let her know that I'm here.

As I reach the door, she's already there, pulling it open as if she were waiting there for me. A smile touches my lips as my eyes scan over her. She's dressed in a pair of sweatpants and a hoodie, her face free of any makeup and her raven-colored hair pulled up in a messy bun on top of her head.

"Hey," she says softly, as she steps out of the way for me to enter. "Sorry about the library. I didn't know about it until last minute and I meant to text you but I ended up taking a quick nap and didn't remember until it was time for us to meet."

"You don't have to apologize," I tell her, smiling down at her as she shuts the door behind me. "It's not like it was that far of a drive. And this is the first time you've ever invited me over here."

She shifts her weight nervously, reaching up to tighten her bun as she heads deeper into the apart-ment. "Well, I don't know. It's a pretty small place, so I didn't really think you would want to come here."

I follow her through the small kitchen that leads into an open-floor plan. Her apartment is a studio with the living room and bedroom combined. Even though it's essentially all one room, it's a larger space than she implied. Her bed is tucked over in its own little nook and the living room is practically separate with how much space is between the two areas.

"It's not small," I tell her, my voice gentle as we walk over to the couch. Aspen takes a seat and I sit down next to her, not bothering to move as my thigh brushes against hers. "Plus, I don't give a shit what it looks like. You could live in a cardboard box and it would still feel like home."

I watch as a pink tint spreads across her cheeks and she ducks her head for a moment, leaning forward to grab her book. I don't know why I said the words, especially when I need to cut this rope that is threading itself between us. But it's not a lie. Aspen has a way of making everywhere feel like home, as long as she's there. Her presence alone does something to me and I can't bring myself to put the feeling into words because that will only solidify what I've been trying to avoid.

I'm fucking falling for this girl and I can't let myself go there.

"So, I don't know what you really want to go over," she admits honestly as she pulls her legs up onto the couch and sits cross-legged. "I know we don't have any exams coming until next week and things have been pretty easy in class. Do you feel like you have a decent understanding of what we've been learning?"

Swallowing hard, I glance over at her as she stares at me expectantly. I can either tell her the truth, that I don't need her help anymore, or I can lie just to keep her around. "I think I'm good with everything we've been learning," I admit, choosing to go with honesty rather than lying.

Aspen narrows her eyes for a moment, but then her face relaxes as she tilts her head to the side. "If you didn't want to study, then why did you still want to meet?"

Fuck. I should have known this would be her follow-up question, but I'm not sure that I'm fully prepared to answer it. I'm stuck in another position where I could either choose to lie or be honest. Aspen at least deserves the truth... even if it might hurt her in the end.

"Because I haven't been able to stop thinking

about you since last weekend," I admit, my voice low and hoarse as I focus on the small golden specks in her irises. "I wanted to see you outside of class. Away from all the bullshit in life."

She stares back at me with a heated gaze, her tongue slowly wetting her lips. "Like a distraction?"

The corners of my lips lift and I nod. "That's what friends are for, right?"

A soft laugh escapes her as I enter her space, pushing her back down into the couch as I hover above her. Aspen's lips part slightly, a ragged breath falling from her mouth as I stare down at her. She really is fucking breathtaking and that's why I know I have to end this. This girl has situated herself too fucking deep and I need to extract her from my soul.

My face dips down to hers as I steal her breath, my mouth colliding with hers. Aspen wraps her arms around the back of my neck, her tongue sliding along mine as we deepen the kiss and I let her in. This has to be the last time and because of that, I'm going to worship her like she deserves before I rip her heart to shreds.

Pulling away, I trail my lips along the underside of her jaw and down the side of her neck. Her nails dig into my shoulders as I push her shirt up and move my mouth across her skin. Aspen's legs fall to the sides, giving me full access as I make my way down her body. Sliding my fingers under the waistband of her sweats, I begin to pull them down as she lifts her head to look at me.

"What are you doing?" she questions me, her voice filled with panic as she involuntarily lifts her hips for me to slide down her pants and underwear.

A smirk plays on my lips and I look up at her as I peel her clothes from her body, leaving her exposed from the waist down. "I wanna make you feel good, baby. I want to taste that sweet pussy on my tongue."

Aspen pulls her bottom lip in between her teeth, biting down as I drag my tongue along her pussy. A moan falls from her lips, her head tipping back as she lets herself fall back onto the couch. This is the first time we've been intimate in this way and it fucking pains me that this will be the last time I get to taste her pleasure.

Sliding my tongue along her, I take my time, tasting every inch before nipping at her clit. Aspen's hands are in my hair, fisting my locks as I grip her thighs, holding her in place while devouring her. Her hips buck every time I press my tongue against her clit and I smile against her as I continue my slow assault, teasing her with every lick.

I work my mouth against her, swirling my tongue around her clit as she cries out. Her body shakes as I drive her closer and closer to the edge. She's captivating and has me so fucking wrapped up in her, I can't even think straight. All I can think about is Aspen and how badly I need her in my life right now.

But that's somewhere I can't allow myself to go. As badly as I want to, I can't let her into my life any more than she already is. And the only way to make all of this stop is to erase her from my life completely. I just know this is going to fucking hurt, but I can't focus on that right now.

The only thing I need to be focusing on is this moment—this moment with her that I never want to end.

Aspen is so close, her voice hoarse as she calls out. She wraps her fingers around my locks of hair, tugging on me as she fights against me to clamp her thighs around my head. Sliding my forearms against her legs, I pin her down and move my mouth against her, flicking her clit with my tongue over and over again.

Flattening my tongue, I press it against her, applying pressure as I pull one arm away from her leg and slowly slide my finger inside her. Aspen's hips buck, her thigh pressing against the side of my head as I push her over the edge. She's falling, fucking losing herself as she comes on my tongue. She sounds like an angel, calling out my name, and tastes like the heavens above.

Sliding my tongue along her, I lick her, tasting every last drop as she rides out her high. Her body shakes, her thighs clamped around my head, her fingers still wrapped up in my hair as she drifts into the abyss of ecstasy.

Pulling my finger from her wet pussy, I lift my head, peering up at her from between her legs. I slowly sit up and she lifts her head, her eyebrows drawing together as her eyes scan me.

"Why are you still dressed?" she questions me, tilting her head to the side.

"You want me naked, baby girl?" I ask her, rising to my feet with her eyes following me. "Why don't you tell me what it is you want?"

A fire burns in her hooded gaze as she stares up at me. "I want you inside me, Cam. I want you to fuck me."

A smirk forms on my lips as I reach behind my head and grab the collar of my shirt. Pulling it over my head, I toss it onto the floor before reaching for the waistband of my sweatpants. I shove them down my thighs, taking my boxers along with them before they fall to the floor, pooling around my feet. Stepping out of them, I bend down to grab a condom from my pocket and tear it open with my teeth.

Aspen's eyes are on me, greedy as fuck as she drinks me in. Positioning myself between her legs, I slide the condom over my cock and press the tip against her pussy. Aspen's hands claw at my back, urging me forward as I slowly push inside her.

A moan falls from her lips, her eyes rolling back in her head as I fill her to the brim with my cock. Dropping my hands onto the couch beside her head, I bring my lips down to her ear, nipping at her lobe. "I'm going to fuck you until my name is the only word you fucking remember," I murmur, dragging my tongue along the outer shell of her ear.

Sliding one hand down to her ass, my fingertips dig into her flesh as I grip her in my palm. Thrusting my hips, I pound into her, fucking her harder and faster with every thrust. This wasn't supposed to be a race, I was supposed to take my time and enjoy her, but fuck that.

Right now, all I want to feel is her coming around my cock as I lose myself deep inside her. The rest can come later, because I plan on fucking her all night long.

Aspen claws at my back, her fingernails digging into my skin as she runs them along my flesh. I pound into her harder and harder as she wraps her legs around my waist. My mouth collides with hers as a rush of warmth spreads across my stomach and through my body. I'm so fucking close and I can feel that she is, too, with the way her pussy grips my cock.

I steal the air from her lungs, breathing her in as I piston my hips. My balls constrict, drawing closer to my body as I feel my release right on the brink. I pound into her once more, swallowing her moans as she comes completely undone, shattering around me as her orgasm tears through her body.

That's all it takes to send me soaring over the edge with her, free falling into the euphoric abyss. I'm completely consumed and so fucking lost in this girl, I don't want to ever be found.

But I know this can only last for tonight...

And then I have to end things with her.

CHAPTER TWENTY-FOUR
ASPEN

Cameron left early this morning and there was a shift in the air before he left. After the first round, he was gentle and tender and took his time with me all night. I didn't anticipate him staying the night, but once we got started, he stayed until after the sun rose. There was a storm brewing in those cloudy green eyes of his before he went home.

He didn't say much, but I could feel the shift and I wasn't sure how to interpret it. The last thing I want to do is read into anything, but I don't know that I can help myself. He left with the promise of calling me later in the day and I wasn't holding my breath to wait for him to actually call.

I haven't left my bed much today, except to take

a shower. My body was sore from the marathon Cam and I did last night and I needed something to help ease the pain in my muscles. I was supposed to go to my classes, but I've been doing well enough that I could afford to skip a day. Plus, I have someone in each of my classes that can send me the notes for the material I've missed for the day.

Delilah called me not long after I slipped back under the covers of my bed, asking me where I was. I told her I was at home, too tired to come in today, so that was all she needed to invite herself over to dig and see what was going on.

She knows me well enough to know that I don't take many mental health days and that's what I told her today was. Crawling out of my bed, I wrap a blanket around myself and head over to unlock the door for her. I grab a water bottle from the fridge on my way back through the apartment before settling on the couch instead of in bed.

After flipping through the channels, I settle on some garbage reality TV show to mindlessly get lost in until she gets here. It doesn't take long for Delilah to show up and I already know that she opted out of going to her two afternoon classes to get the scoop on what was going on with me instead.

Delilah walks into the apartment, shutting the

door behind her before finding me on the couch. She drops down onto the other side, lying down as she props herself up with a pillow. I glance over at her, acknowledging her presence as she quietly says hey, as if she's treading lightly and is unsure how to approach whatever the situation could potentially be.

We sit in silence for a few moments, just staring at the TV before she abruptly sits up and faces me. "Okay, if you're not going to tell me what's going on, you've left me no choice but to ask instead." She pauses for a moment, her eyebrows pulling together as she tilts her head to the side. "What's up, Asp? It's not like you to miss classes like this, so you better spill, girl."

A sigh slips from my lips as I roll over onto my side to face her. I don't bother moving off the couch or sitting up as I continue to lay there. "Cam came over and spent the night last night and I'm not sure how I feel about it."

That's a lie because I know exactly how I feel about it, I just don't know that I'm ready to admit it out loud.

"What do you mean?" she questions me, her eyes filled with curiosity, and I know it's killing her to not get all the dirty details of our night together.

"This wasn't the first night you guys spent together, right?"

I shake my head. "No, I've stayed at his place a few times, but this time it was different. When he left this morning, something just felt off and it left me unsettled."

"How was he last night while he was here?"

Swallowing hard, our time together replays in my head. "He was different then too. Almost as if there was something more to it than fucking around... I don't know how to explain it. He was just super attentive to my needs and making sure that I felt good and was taken care of."

"Holy fuck," Delilah breathes, her eyes widening as she shakes her head in disbelief. "It felt different because it was more than fucking around. He's got it bad, girl, and you fucking know it."

"No," I shake my head, refusing to accept her statement. "We had an agreement. No feelings, no attachments. It wasn't supposed to end up this way..." My voice trails off for a moment as I stare back at her. "I wasn't supposed to get attached to him."

Delilah stares back at me in disbelief. "You're finally admitting this shit? Because I could have told you it was going to happen. With the way the two of you have been spending time together, the way you light up with him around. It's so obvious you're falling for him."

"I can't, Delilah. I can't allow that to happen... but I think it's too late."

Delilah sighs, a small frown forming on her lips. "Are you going to tell him? You said something felt off when he left this morning?"

"I don't know if I should tell him. This morning, he was different than he was last night. Almost as if he were trying to put distance between us. He didn't really hang around that long after he woke up and said he'd call me later, but I don't know that I believe that."

"Shit," Delilah breathes, shaking her head. "I can't believe you actually caught feelings for him." She pauses, tapping her chin for a moment. "Maybe give him some space because it sounds like he might be freaked out too. I don't know, girl. Both of you are so against having feelings for someone, I don't see this ending well."

My stomach sinks as a wave of nausea rolls through me. There's no way this can end well because we're going against everything we had talked about not happening. And what if Cameron doesn't have feelings for me? What if he could just tell that I've gotten attached and that's pushing him away?

"What am I supposed to do, Delilah?" I ask her, my voice desperate for some kind of guidance. I'm stuck in a place I've never been in before and I literally have no idea of how to proceed. "Is it even worth saying anything to him when I already know this is going to blow up in my face? I mean, with how devoted he is to hockey, he would never have time for a relationship anyways. And I need to focus on getting into med school."

Delilah shrugs. "I literally don't have a good answer to that question, babe. I think you should just keep it to yourself for now. Just separate yourself, put some distance between the two of you and almost detach from the entire thing. I think if you can go back to focusing on this being a temporary situation, an arrangement that ends when the semester does, you will be okay."

"You're right," I agree, nodding as I roll onto my back and direct my gaze back to the TV. "I can't tell Cameron. I can't let myself feel any of this. I just need to bury it and lock it away so it can never resurface again."

"Exactly," Delilah agrees. "Fuck Cameron Sawyer. You're going to be a bad-ass doctor and all that he is, is a distraction. Cut ties with his ass as soon as the semester is over."

Her words ring in my head and I know she's right. As much as it hurts to admit, it's my own stupid fault. I shouldn't have let my guard down and let him get close. Feelings were the last thing I was supposed to catch, and here I am now.

I fucked around and got attached.

And now I need to figure out how to detach myself from the one person my heart desires.

CHAPTER TWENTY-FIVE
CAMERON

I've been successfully able to avoid seeing Aspen outside of class and it's honestly been killing me. Things have shifted between us and it's all my fault. After I spent the night with her last week, I found myself in the exact situation I have been trying to not get caught up in since I started having an interest in girls.

And Aspen managed to switch the game up on me. She nestled herself inside my soul and I can't have her in there. Our futures don't match up. After she graduates next year, she's going to med school and I'm off to hopefully play in the NHL. Neither of us will have time for a relationship, so this is literally a waste of time.

We can't continue fucking around and keep

things on a friendship level with the way our dynamic has shifted. I'm too far gone with her and I need to pull myself from the depths of her ocean before I completely drown in her waters.

I've canceled on her for the past week for our tutoring sessions. Between hockey and the mind-fuck that I've been dealing with, I needed some space to think and the only way I was going to get that was by putting some distance between the two of us. Being around her clouds my thoughts and makes it that much harder to come to the conclusion I needed to come to.

I have no choice but to end things with Aspen.

And hope that one day, she'll thank me, even though I know it's going to break her heart... and mine.

We're supposed to meet at the library at seven and surprisingly Aspen is strolling in the room as I walk through the main doors of the building. I watch her from a distance, the way she moves through the room like she's floating on air. She's fucking ethereal and goddamn—this is going to be harder than I had imagined.

Taking a deep breath, I walk farther inside the library. Aspen is sitting at the table we normally meet at, but she doesn't have any of her materials spread across the wooden surface. It surprises me and honestly throws me off as I walk over toward her.

Aspen types something on her phone, lifting her gaze to mine as I stop at the table she's seated at. Instead of sitting next to her, I take the seat across from her, putting more distance between us, because fuck... I can't be close to her right now or it's going to derail my plan completely.

I watch her face as confusion washes through her eyes, her eyebrows pulling together slightly before her guard goes back into place. She pushes her shoulders back, squaring them as she stares at me with curiosity.

"Aren't we studying?" I ask her, my voice strained. Clearing my throat, I make an attempt to swallow back the emotion that is building, but it doesn't fully help.

Aspen stares back at me. "Is there something in particular that you wanted to go over? We haven't met in, like, a week, so I wasn't sure if this was actually about studying or what was going on."

I swallow roughly, my jaw clenching momentarily as I take in her challenging look. She's not pleased with me and there's a coldness that radiates from her, chilling me to the bone. I'm used to the cold—I practically live on the ice—and that doesn't come close to the frigidness that encapsulates Aspen right now.

"You're right, this isn't about studying," I start, my voice low as I fold my arms over one another on the table. "I'm sorry for canceling on you and not really reaching out lately. My hockey schedule has been pretty demanding and since my grades have been better, I needed to put my sole focus on practice instead."

"You don't owe me any explanations, Cameron," she says dismissively, her voice void of any emotion as she stares at me blankly. "You have your life and I have mine. Whether you choose to need my help anymore is your prerogative."

Fuck. I don't even know how to go about this. We're not in a relationship but I can't help but feel like I'm breaking up with her. I don't do feelings, I don't do any of this shit. A clean break is going to be better than dragging this out. We can't continue doing this, point-blank.

"I think we need to keep our friendship as strictly just friends. And studying," I tell her, my voice hoarse as I stare back into her ice glazed eyes. "The whole benefits thing isn't working out for me."

I watch her throat bob as she swallows, a wave

of pain passing through her irises, but she quickly recovers as she nods. "I agree. I don't think it's working for either of us and it's better if we just end it now instead of waiting until the end of the semester."

Her words catch me off guard and I sit back in my chair, crossing my arms over my chest. My brow furrows and I tilt my head to the side as I stare back at the contradiction that she is. I didn't expect her to break down and fall apart in front of me, but she's sitting here agreeing with me.

What the fuck is happening right now?

And why the fuck does this hurt so badly?

The way she's staring at me, with a coldness I've never experienced from her, shakes me to my core. This isn't the Aspen I've grown close to. This is the Aspen who wants to push me away too. And fuck me for wanting to push back. Her words linger in my mind, playing on repeat. She wants to end this between us and it feels like she's ripping my heart from my chest.

"So, we have an agreement then?" I ask her, my voice sounding like it's miles away. Hell, it doesn't even sound like it's coming from my body right now. "We go back to just being friends."

Aspen frowns, shaking her head at me. "I don't

think that that's going to work for me either," she admits, her voice low and harsh. "I can't tutor you anymore, Cameron. We crossed a line when we shifted into friends with benefits and there's no going back now. What's done is done and we can't take it back. All that we can do is move forward in the opposite directions that we're going."

I stare back at her, words completely failing me. This was completely unexpected and I don't know how the hell to recover from this right now. This isn't where I wanted this to go. I still want her in my life, just at arm's length instead of entangled around my heart.

Grabbing her bag, she rises to her feet and tucks her phone in the back pocket of her jeans. "If you need someone else to tutor you, reach out to Jenna in our class. She'll be able to help you. And maybe you can squeeze some benefits out of that new friendship then too."

Aspen slices her eyes to me and I see the fucking pain she's currently swimming in. She does a good job, putting on a cold front, but I see right through her facade. She only agreed with me because I suggested it first. And there's no doubt in my mind that her heart is aching the same way mine is right now.

"Wait, Aspen," I call after her as she spins on her heel and begins to stride through the library. I quickly climb out of my chair, my feet scrambling as I chase after her. "That's not what any of this was. I don't do this shit with everyone."

As her hand reaches for the handle on the door, she glances at me over her shoulder. "Save it, Cam. I honestly don't fucking care what you do. None of it is any of my business. Good luck with the rest of the semester and hockey season."

My lips part, my mouth falling open as I watch her disappear through the doorway. I should stop her and tell her I didn't mean any of it, but I can't bring myself to go after her. Things are better off this way. Like she said, she has her life and I have mine.

This was supposed to end eventually anyway.

I just didn't expect it to hurt this badly.

CHAPTER TWENTY-SIX
ASPEN

It's been two weeks since the arrangement between Cam and I ended. It affected me in a way I never had imagined that it would. I knew I was treading in deep waters that I didn't belong in. I had broken my number one rule and found myself falling for him. Thankfully, Cameron was able to end it for both our sakes, because I don't know that I would have been able to.

Even though I agreed with him, there was a reluctance that I didn't let show. I could tell it caught him off guard when I simply just gave in and went along with what he was saying. It confused me more than anything—because it almost seemed like he wanted me to fight against him. But how could I possibly fight for something that was never supposed to exist in the first place?

I didn't want the feelings any more than he did. But now that we ruined and lost our friendship in the midst of it all, I can't help but feel fucking worse. Not only did I lose the one person my heart desired, I also lost someone who I had grown close to. *A real friend.* The sex was an added bonus, but I genuinely enjoyed his company and spending time with him.

None of that matters now, because it's all fucking gone. And now I'm just left with my own feelings and wallowing in my sorrows. I had never cried over a guy before until Cam. It was my own fault for letting myself get as involved with him as I did. I shouldn't have spent as much time with him. If we would have just kept things physical, maybe there wouldn't have been any attachment between the two of us.

Instead, I let my guard down and I let him in. Hell, I even told him about my ADHD diagnosis and medication. That's something that even Delilah doesn't know about and she's my best friend. Cameron forced his way under my skin and then removed himself like he was simply ripping off a Band-Aid. What he didn't realize was he took a piece of me with him. The very organ that beats inside of my chest.

Now, it's just a shattered mess, barely beating inside my rib cage.

"Aspen," Delilah's voice sounds from the other side of my apartment door as she bangs her fist on it. "I know you're in there and you better open this goddamn door before I break it down."

Sighing, I roll onto my side and sit up on the edge of my bed. I know Delilah well enough to know that she means what she's saying. She may not be physically able to break down the door, but she will try with all of her might. And probably piss off all of my neighbors in the process.

I've been ignoring her texts and calls since yesterday. It's Saturday and I just want to spend the evening in bed, like I have been for the past two weeks. It's not like I cut her off when all of this happened. She's seen me at school, but other than that, I've shut her out. I just don't have the will to entertain anyone right now.

And when she noticed the avoidance between Cam and I in class, she didn't hesitate to question me on it. I didn't give her the full explanation, because I wasn't sure I really wanted to speak it into existence. It was easier to just pretend like he didn't exist, even though I had to face him every day. He stopped sitting in the seat next to me and instead found one in the back of the room.

Never once did I chance a glance in his direction because behind me is where he belongs. He's a part of my past now because he was never supposed to be a part of my future.

Delilah keeps banging on the door, muttering obscenities as I shuffle through my kitchen and unlock the deadbolt. As I pull open the door, her fist is still in the air, but she quickly drops it when she sees me standing in front of her.

"Jesus, when was the last time you showered or changed your clothes?" she questions me, her face scrunching up as she takes in my appearance. I glance down at my tattered terry cloth shorts and my faded band t-shirt. My hair is a knotted mess on the top of my head, probably because I haven't brushed it in a few days.

Shrugging, I step out of the way so she can slide past me into the apartment. I close the door behind her and move around her as she pauses in the kitchen. She glances over at the sink, which is filled with some dishes that have been sitting there for a few days.

Yeah, I may have been neglecting my own

appearance, along with all of my household chores. Fucking sue me. I guess this is what a broken heart will do to you.

Delilah follows me into the main part of my apartment, but I continue walking over to my bed and crawl back under the covers into the exact place I was when she was pounding on my door. Luckily from my bed, I can see the TV which is playing some sappy Hallmark movie. I don't know why I've been watching them, but seeing other people in love reminds me that not all hope is lost.

Although, it really is.

Love isn't something I wanted before... until I found myself falling for Cam.

But I'm not sure I ever want that feeling with someone else.

Delilah sighs, kicking off her shoes as she shrugs out of her coat and tosses it onto the back of the couch along with her purse. She walks over to my bed, to the empty side, and climbs under the covers with me. I can feel her warmth as she shifts on the mattress, her body occupying the space that Cam once did.

"Aspen," she says softly as she tucks a pillow under her head. I can feel her gaze on the back of my head, but I keep staring over at the TV instead. "I'm really worried about you. I've never seen you like this before and have no idea what to do to help you."

"There's nothing you can do," I tell her, shrugging with indifference as I roll onto my back. My gaze lands on the ceiling and I trace invisible patterns in the white paint. "Cam and I talked about it and even though he was the one who suggested it, I agreed, so I guess it was a mutual decision."

Turning my head to the side, I meet Delilah's perplexed gaze as her eyebrows pull together. "What do you mean it was a mutual decision? I didn't push for answers before when you said things were done between the two of you, but you have to give me more than that, girl. I know it hurts, but maybe it will feel better to talk about it."

Swallowing hard over the emotions that builds in my throat, I nod slowly. "He said that the friends with benefits thing wasn't working for him and I agreed because it wasn't for me either. You called me out on my feelings for him and it made me realize that I didn't want the same arrangement with him that we already had. So, when he told me it wasn't working for him, I had no choice but to agree."

Delilah raises an eyebrow. "You didn't ask him what he meant by that or what had changed?"

"It didn't matter. He spoke his piece and I wasn't about to spill my feelings for him then. I had to let it go and let him go. Let's be real here, Delilah," I start, the exasperation evident in my voice. "We live two separate lives. We're heading in two different directions. It would never work. And telling him how I felt wouldn't have changed a single fucking thing."

"Damn, girl," Delilah breathes, her eyes sympathetic as they search mine, and she frowns. "I'm so sorry. I really thought he was feeling the same way about you with the way things were between the two of you. I hope you told him that you were done helping him study. Fuck him," she sneers, curling her lip up in disgust. "I hope he fails without your help."

A soft laugh falls from my lips and it sounds foreign. I don't remember the last time that I laughed like this. "Okay, let's not be dramatic. I don't want to see him do badly in life. I just know I can't be a part of his life... not even as friends."

"Well, good for you, because you deserve more than that bullshit. And you definitely don't deserve to sit in the fucking friend zone." Delilah stares back at me, a sinister smile curling on her lips as she quickly sits up. "Enough of this self-pity shit, Asp. I've given you enough time to wallow in your sorrows. You know the best way to get over someone is to get under someone else."

Narrowing my eyes at her, my nostrils flare as I shake my head. I'm not ready to hop on someone else like Cameron never happened.

"Okay, fine," she says, rolling her eyes as she rises to her feet and pulls the covers away from my body. She discards them on the floor and I glare up at her as I sit up in bed. "Go shower and clean yourself up. We're going out tonight and having a good time. Cameron Sawyer is not worth your fucking time and you've wasted enough energy with him breaking your heart."

"I don't want to go out, Delilah."

She shakes her finger at me, simultaneously shaking her head. "I'm not taking no for an answer. Either you wash the filth off or I'm dragging you out looking like you just crawled out of a dumpster."

A sigh slips from my lips and I rise to my feet, my eyes still narrowed at her. Delilah is too persistent and I know she isn't going to give up. She has a point, though. I've wasted far too much of my energy thinking about Cameron. Maybe going out will be good to get my mind off him. And I could definitely use a shower.

"You know, you're cruel," I sneer at her, catching

clean clothes as she tosses them to me from my drawers and closet.

Delilah puts her hands on her hips, grinning at me with satisfaction. "I know, but you'll thank me later for this." She strolls toward me, grabbing my shoulders as she spins me around and starts to push me toward the bathroom. "There's a party going on tonight and we're going."

Another sigh falls from my lips as she practically shoves me into the bathroom and pulls the door shut behind me. Dropping all of my clothes onto the counter, I look at myself in the mirror for the first time all day and cringe at my appearance. She was right. I look like shit, like a shell of a person.

I don't know what kind of spell Cameron put on me, but it's time that I get rid of it tonight. This doesn't erase the pain that still lingers in the fibers of my heart, but it's a start. It's a step in the right direction, of getting over him and moving forward in life.

We all have to start somewhere, right?

And this is me starting to live my life after Cameron Sawyer came in and shook everything up.

CHAPTER TWENTY-SEVEN
CAMERON

Sitting on the couch, I drop my controller down onto the coffee table and glance over at Hayden and Simon. They're still bickering over the video game we were playing. I ended up beating both of them for the third time tonight and each time, they've found reasons to blame the other for messing up their chances at winning. Either that or I got blamed for cheating.

"You done playing?" Simon asks me when he notices my controller sitting on the table. "We can play a different game if you want to instead."

Shaking my head, I rise to my feet and walk out of the living room. "I'm tired of playing video games, honestly. I appreciate the two of you trying to get me out of this funk, but seriously. I'm fine."

Simon's phone begins to ring, just as Hayden follows me into the kitchen and grabs a beer from the fridge. He takes the bottle opener from the counter and pops off the top of his bottle before taking a swig. Leaning against the countertop, his eyes find mine as I stare at him from the other side of the room.

"What?" I ask him, narrowing my eyes as I feel uncomfortable under his gaze. I haven't talked to any of the guys about what happened with Aspen, but I know they have noticed her absence and me being around more often.

Hayden tilts his head to the side. "You gonna tell me what's going on? And don't bother trying to bull-shit me, man. I know it has to do with Aspen."

Narrowing my eyes at him, I walk past him and grab a beer, mimicking him as I pop the top off with the bottle opener. I take a large gulp, my glare still meeting his gaze. "What makes you think it has anything to do with her?"

"Because I'm not fucking stupid," he snaps at me, shaking his head. "Dude, you were practically wifed up like Knight and Whitley. And now you're around all the time, acting like someone killed your puppy dog, and she hasn't been around at all. I haven't asked because I didn't want to pry, but seriously, bro. We're best friends—you're like my brother—you can talk to me about shit."

"Did it ever occur to you that maybe I didn't want to talk about it?" I quip, taking another sip of my beer.

"Obviously," he says, rolling his eyes. "We're both the same way. We shut everyone out and don't let anyone know what's really going on. But you're not acting like yourself at all and everyone can tell, dude."

"Fine," I sigh, shaking my head as I run a frustrated hand through my hair. "I ended shit with her. The friends with benefits shit was a terrible fucking idea and I couldn't let it go any further."

"Because you were starting to have feelings for her."

Slicing my eyes at Hayden, I stare at him, my nostrils flaring as he speaks the words into the universe. I hate the truth behind them because I know that I fucked it all up now. But fuck him for being right.

"Yeah," I admit, my voice dropping as I cast my gaze to the floor. My hand is in my hair again and I spin around to set my beer down on the counter. "I really think that I fucked up, Hayden."

"You regret ending shit with her now?"

Glancing back at him, his eyes are filled with nothing but sympathy as he stares at me with curiosity. A frown works its way onto my lips and I nod. "I was scared of how I was feeling. Scared for what the future would bring or how things wouldn't work out between us... but I think I made the wrong choice. Instead of being afraid of my feelings, I should have been honest with her but I pushed her away."

"How did she react to it?" Hayden questions me, taking another sip of his beer as he continues to lazily lean against the counter.

"That's the thing that confused me more than anything. She agreed and was all about cutting off the benefits. But then she decided that we couldn't even be friends." I pause for a moment, the look in her eyes haunting me like it has for the past two weeks. "It's like she changed before my eyes into this cold, closed-off version of the girl I fell in love with."

"Because you broke her heart, bro," Hayden informs me, his voice barely audible. He shakes his head at me. "She didn't want you to think it affected her when it really did. Have you talked to her since?"

"No," I admit, grabbing my beer as I take

another swig. "I moved seats and everything to give her space. She won't even fucking look at me, man."

Hayden purses his lips. "Why would she want to? If she's trying to get over you, seeing you is only going to make it worse."

"Fuck," I mumble, running my hand down my face. "What do I do, Hayden?"

"You go get your girl."

Nodding, I pull out my phone as my heart pounds erratically in my chest. I scroll through my contacts and find her name. My finger hovers for a moment as I question whether or not I'm making another mistake. What if she doesn't want anything to do with me after this? Can I really blame her for it after I broke her heart?

Instead of sending her a message, I tap on the phone button next to her name and call her. Lifting my phone to my ear, I listen as it rings. And rings. And rings. My stomach falls, dread rolling in the pit of my abdomen as my call goes to voicemail.

I don't know what I was expecting, thinking that she would actually answer. And I can't blame her for that either. Why would she want to talk to me? If I were her, I wouldn't give myself the time of day at all.

"She didn't answer," I tell Hayden as I set my phone down on the counter.

He narrows his eyes at me. "Jesus, what is wrong with you? You're really going to give up that easily? You called her one time and she didn't answer. Call her again, text her, go off the rails like a psycho and fucking stalk her down. Do something other than stand here with your thumb up your ass like you don't know what to do."

"Well, how the hell am I supposed to find her if she isn't answering her phone, Hayden?"

"Um, start with social media?" He says it with annoyance like it's the most obvious thing I should have thought of. "Look," he says, pulling out his phone as he opens Instagram. He goes to Aspen's profile, to which there are no new posts or stories. "She hasn't posted anything, so maybe she's at home. But first, we have to check her friend's just in case."

I watch over Hayden's shoulder as he goes to Delilah's page and see that she has a new story. He clicks on it and we go through the first two that are just little quotes about life and happiness. The next one is a picture of herself dressed up to go out, and then there's one of her and Aspen at what looks to be a party.

My heart stops in my chest and I glance up at Hayden. His eyebrows are raised and a slow smile creeps onto his lips. He clicks it again and there's a video of Aspen dancing with a drink in hand and a guy who is too close for fucking comfort.

"What the fuck?"

"See," he smirks, holding his finger on the screen as he peers at his phone. "They're at Danny's house. I heard he was having a party. All it takes is a little detective work and boom, there's your girl."

I stare back at him, my blood boiling as I glance back at his phone. "Are you driving or am I?"

"There's my boy," he smiles, clapping his hand on my back as he abandons the rest of his beer. "I'll drive."

———

We pull up out in front of Danny's house and Hayden barely has the car in park before I'm climbing out. He parks it along the street and kills the engine, not far behind me as I stroll into the house. My eyes are wild, glancing around as I step into the house, looking for any sign of Aspen.

"Chill out, dude," Hayden practically yells in my ear over the music. "You can't go in here like a fucking caveman. Let's get a drink and we'll make our rounds and find her. You don't want to scare her off after being the one who pushed her away in the first place. You gotta play the game the right way."

Glancing over at him, a sinister smirk plays on my lips. "And I always play to fucking win."

I follow Hayden into the kitchen and he grabs both of us beers from the fridge. Twisting off the top, I take a gulp before glancing around the room. Aspen is nowhere to be found. Hayden's eyes trail around after mine, his gaze meeting mine as he shrugs and motions for us to head out through the doorway to his left.

We both walk through and end up in the living room where it's completely packed with people dancing. Standing along the perimeter, my eyes travel over the different heads bobbing and bodies moving until the air leaves my lungs. Aspen is on the other side of the room, holding her cup in the air as she moves against the guy standing behind her. She's wearing a pair of tight black leggings and a cropped tank top.

My eyes drop down to her waist and I see his hands gripping her flesh as he moves against her. All I see is red... blood fucking red.

"Cam, wait," Hayden calls out after me, but his

voice doesn't even come close to touching the logical part of my brain. All that I can see is Aspen and the dude behind her. And there's no way in hell that this is happening.

Pushing through the crowd, I don't stop moving until I'm standing directly in front of her. Her eyes are closed as she moves along to the music, like she's somewhere other than in this room. The guy behind her stops moving as he notices me, his gaze finding mine over her shoulder, and he narrows his eyes at me before leaning toward her ear, saying something to her.

Aspen's eyes flash open, widening as they meet my heated gaze. Her throat bobs as she swallows hard. Completely disregarding the guy behind her, she leaves him as she steps closer to me, drawn to me like a moth to a flame.

And I hope she's ready to burn.

CHAPTER TWENTY-EIGHT
ASPEN

The air leaves my lungs in a rush and I'm almost positive I'm hallucinating. I've had a few drinks, but there's no way I'm this drunk. Or maybe someone slipped something into my drink, because there's no way this can be real right now. Cameron isn't supposed to be here, yet he's standing directly in front of me looking like he's about to commit murder.

Stepping toward him, my mouth feels dry and it feels as if the room is closing in on me. My body sways as the alcohol courses through my system and I reach out, chancing a touch to see if he's real. My hand lands on his warm cheek and his skin feels soft beneath my fingers as I stroke his flesh.

"You're really here," I murmur, my voice barely

audible over the music that pounds through the speakers around the room. I'm not hallucinating. Cam is here in the flesh.

He stares down at me with a fire burning in his eyes. "I am," he says, his voice hoarse and laced with pain. "Where did your friend go?"

My eyebrows tug together and I tilt my head to the side. "Delilah? I don't know, I haven't seen her for a while."

Cam shakes his head at me. "Not her. That asshole who had his hands on you." He looks past me, his eyes distant. "I'd like to break his fucking hands for touching you."

My heart pounds erratically in my chest as the anger rolls off him in waves. Reacting, I reach out and take his hand in mine, squeezing it tightly until his gaze falls back to mine. "I don't know who he is," I tell him honestly. "I was just dancing and he came up and started dancing with me."

His eyes bounce back and forth between mine. "I believe you," he breathes after a moment, his face dipping down to mine as he presses his lips next to my ear. "Can we go somewhere and talk?"

Closing my eyes, I inhale his scent, reveling in how close he is to me right now. God, I missed him more than I had ever wanted to admit. And blame it on the alcohol, because my guard is completely down and I don't know how to put it back in place right now.

I nod as he pulls away and he laces his fingers in mine, his palm warming my skin as he leads me through the house. We pass Hayden, who smiles at me as our eyes meet. He stands off to the side, slowly sipping his beer as Cam takes me through the doorway, leading me to the back door.

We step outside into the darkness of the night and the air is cold against my skin. I left my coat somewhere inside and I drop his hand as I wrap my arms around myself. Even with the alcohol, I still feel colder than I had anticipated. Cam stares at me for a moment, frowning before he shrugs off his coat and wraps it around my shoulders.

I slip my hands through the holes for the arms, feeling his warmth as I wrap it around my body. Cam stares at me for a moment, his expression unreadable as his eyes desperately search mine. Wrapping an arm around my shoulders, he leads me over to a chair and pulls it out for me to sit down. I drop down onto it, feeling the heaviness in my body as Cam drags another chair in front of me and sits on it.

"I fucked up, Aspen," he breathes, his voice low

and filled with emotion as a wave of pain passes through his eyes.

"What do you mean?" I ask him, the panic in me building as my mind races with possible scenarios of what could have possibly happened. "Are you in trouble? Did something happen?"

He tilts his head to the side, a chuckle rumbling in his chest. "No, nothing like that," he says, easing my anxiety as he stares directly through me. "I fucked up with you because I couldn't be honest with myself."

Swallowing hard, I wrap my arms tighter around my body as I stare back at him. My lips part slightly, but no words find me as I'm taken aback by his admission. Even with the alcohol in my system, I'm coherent enough to understand what he's saying and I'm afraid of where he's going with this.

"I'm not going to lie to you, I'm still fucking scared, but I shouldn't have acted on that fear in the way I did. I shouldn't have ruined things between us because I was afraid of my feelings for you—because I found myself falling for you."

I stare back at him, my breath catching in my throat as my heart pounds erratically in my chest. "You're not the only one who made a mistake because of their feelings," I admit quietly, my eyes bouncing back and forth between his. "Even though it broke my heart, I went along with it because I was afraid too."

Cam's expression softens under the glow of the light that hangs above the back door behind us. There aren't many people lingering out here, given how cold the air has grown as it's gotten later in the night. My heart cracks as I admit the truth to him— that he wasn't the only one who made a mistake that day.

"Come here, baby," he murmurs, both of his arms stretched out to me.

Rising to my feet, my body sways slightly from the liquor that I was drinking as I step closer to him. His hands find my hips and he pulls me down onto his lap. Turning to face him, he wraps his arms around my torso, burying his face in my neck as I nestle into his warmth.

"Let me make things right," he murmurs softly, his lips brushing against the tender skin along my neck. "Please, give me a chance to show you that I can be what you deserve. When I said that being friends with benefits wasn't working for me, I wasn't honest with you. I want to be more than just your friend, Aspen. You're all I fucking think about. I

only have eyes for you, baby, and I want you to officially be mine."

My breath catches in my throat and I pull away
from him for a moment. His eyes bounce back and
forth between mine, searching them as a storm of
emotion brews inside his irises. "You want to be
with me... like together, as a couple?"

A ghost of a smile plays on Cam's lips as he nods.
Lifting his hands to my face, he cups my cheeks,
slowly dragging the pad of his thumb across my
bottom lip. "Yes, Aspen. I want you, all of you. I
don't want to play these stupid games anymore.
When I wake up, I want to see your face and when I
go to bed at night, I want you there beside me.
Enough of this friends shit. I want you to be my
girl."

Swallowing hard over the lump that forms in my
throat, a wave of emotion washes over me. My
nostrils flare as the tears prick the corners of my
eyes. Never have I ever felt this way about someone
else before. And as much as it scares me... I want the
same thing with him.

"Are you sure this is what you really want,
Cam?" I ask him, my voice cracking around my
words. "Neither of us are exactly the type to get
involved like this and dive into a relationship."

"I'm ready to dive in, baby," he breathes, his eyes staring directly into my soul. "I want to drown in your ocean and never come up for air again."

Wrapping my hands around the back of his neck, my face dips down to his and he doesn't hesitate as our lips collide. I'm lost in him and if he's ready to drown, then I want to sink to the depths with him. Cam's tongue slides against mine, tasting like beer as he drains the air from my lungs, inhaling my soul as he devours my mouth with his own.

Abruptly, he pulls away from me, both of us breathless as he stares up at me. "I love you, Aspen Rossi. I've been in love with you longer than I've wanted to admit and I know there's no one else for me but you."

My lips part slightly, the emotion welling inside as I stare into his deep green eyes. "I love you, Cameron. I tried not to, but I can't fight it anymore. Even though we both have our separate lives, when I think of my future, I can't imagine it without you."

"Good." He smiles, pulling my face back down to his as his lips brush against mine. "Because you're never going to have to spend a moment of your future without me." He pauses for a moment, nipping at my bottom lip. "Say that you'll be mine, baby."

"I'm yours, Cameron," I breathe, our lips brushing against each other's as our breaths mix together. "I've always been yours and I'll always be yours."

He captures my mouth with his, sealing the deal between us. I'm completely consumed by him, but I know that this is right. We've both fought this longer than we should have and it feels good to finally give in to the inevitable. It's like we're finally free—free to get lost in love with one another.

We tried to fight fate—we tried to fight love...

But in the end, love will always win.

EPILOGUE
CAMERON

Six months later

Standing in August's dining room, I stare across the room, my eyes trained on Aspen as she sits and talks with Poppy and Isla. We've been spending a lot more time with them and honestly, it has been amazing. I finally understand where August and Logan have been coming from this entire time.

I never imagined that I would be committed and tied down to someone the way they were. That was before I found Aspen and before I fell in love with her. Now, I can't imagine a life without her and I never want to spend a day knowing what it feels like after loving her like this.

We've all been having weekly dinners together, but since August and Poppy are still adjusting to life with a baby, we've been coming to their place a lot more often. And alternating with Logan and Isla as far as cooking dinner. Anything we can do to take the pressure off August's and Poppy's shoulders.

It was a huge adjustment for them, bringing a baby into the world. August ended up missing our championship game of the season and it surprised the hell out of me when he didn't even care. We won without him and it didn't affect him one bit because he was completely consumed by Poppy and baby Everett.

Slowly lifting my bottle of beer to my lips, I tip it back as I take a sip, watching as Poppy hands Everett to Aspen. She looks like a natural as she cradles him in her arms like that's exactly where he belongs. Not necessarily him, but a baby.

Our baby.

Seeing her like this gets me every fucking time. We never approached the conversation before, but I want all of this with Aspen. I'm envious of August's life, even though I got the girl of my dreams. It isn't enough because I want more with her.

"She has a way with kids, doesn't she?" August says softly as he steps up beside me. I glance over at him, noting the smile on his lips as he watches my girlfriend holding his baby boy. "When are you gonna wife her up, bro?"

"Yeah, what are you waiting for?" Logan chimes in as he comes and stands with the two of us. "I've gotta be honest, I still can't believe that you're actually in a serious relationship. Like, who the hell would have been able to predict this?"

"Fuck off," I mumble, laughing lightly as I bump my shoulder into his. "I just hadn't found the right girl, until Aspen came into my life."

And isn't that the fucking truth.

It isn't long before Poppy announces that she needs to get Everett into bed and we all take that as our cue to leave. Aspen hands him back over to her and we all say our goodbyes before parting ways for the night. Logan and Isla slip out before us, heading down the hall to their own separate apartment.

Aspen and I ended up getting a place of our own and it's only two blocks away from where Logan and August both live. I considered moving into the same building, but I like my space from the guys now. Especially when I have Aspen who is occupying most of my time.

As we walk out to my car, the night sky is clear with stars sprinkled above us and the moon shining brightly. The air is warm against my skin as we walk hand in hand together. Walking over to the passenger-side door, I pull it open for Aspen and she climbs inside. I close it shut behind her and round the front of the car until I'm climbing into my seat.

Pulling out onto the road, I start heading in the opposite direction of our apartment. Aspen glances over at me, her eyes on the side of my face as she stares at me in curiosity.

"Where are we going?"

Glancing over at her, a smile forms on my lips. "I want to take you somewhere and show you something."

"Okay," she says softly, not asking any more questions. That's one of the things I love about Aspen. She is always down for whatever adventure I want to take her on. And I'm ready to take her on an adventure that is going to last a lifetime.

We drive down the main road, turning off of it onto a back road. It winds through the forest, climbing higher and higher until we reach the top of the cliff. Pulling off on the side of the road, I kill the engine and climb out without saying a word to

Aspen. She's already getting out when I reach her and doesn't hesitate to slip her hand into mine.

I lead her through a small patch of trees until we reach a clearing that looks over the lake down below. It's somewhere the guys and I always come during the winter to shoot pucks when we can't get on the ice at campus.

"What did you want to show me?"

Pointing out at the lake, I look over at her. "This is one of my favorite places. I love it here in the winter, being down there when the lake is frozen and just being in my element with a stick and a puck. But up here is even better. The view of the water below, and if you look up, it's dark enough that you can see every single star in the night sky."

Aspen looks out over the lake before tilting her head back to look up at the stars. "It's absolutely beautiful out here," she breathes, taking in the wonderment of the world beyond us. I'm lost in her and I can't tear my eyes away from her beautiful face.

"It's fucking breathtaking... just like you."

Aspen turns her head to look at me, a soft smile on her lips as her eyes stare through me, deep into my soul. "Thank you for sharing this with me. It's amazing and really makes you realize just how small we are in this world."

"That's not the only thing I want to share with you."

She tilts her head to the side, her eyes widening as I turn to face her, taking both of her hands in mine as I drop down onto one knee in front of her. Aspen takes her hands away from mine, clasping them over her mouth as tears fill her eyes.

Reaching into my pocket, I pull out a small black velvet box. Holding it out to her, I flip open the lid, showing her the diamond ring inside.

"I want to share everything with you, Aspen Rossi. The entire world, the rest of my life. I never want to spend a moment without you and I want you forever, baby. You've become the most important thing to me and I want you to be my wife. To have my babies and share a life with me."

"Cameron..." she chokes out, my name sounding like a sweet melody on her tongue.

"I want to build a future with you. Every fucking part of it. Seeing you with August and Poppy's baby... I want that with you too. I want to watch your stomach grow with our children growing inside you. Share the rest of this life with me, baby, and all of the ones to come after this."

"Of course, I want that with you, Cam," she admits, her voice cracking around her words as the tears spill down her cheeks. "You are my future. And I want nothing more than to build a life and a family with you. If that's not in my future, I don't even want it. You're the love of my life and we were made for each other."

"You possess my heart and my soul, Aspen." A smile forms on my lips, my own tears pricking at the corners of my eyes. "Will you marry me?"

"Yes," she breathes, a soft laugh falling from her lips as the tears continue to fall. "Oh my god, yes!"

Putting out my hand for her, she drops her palm into mine as I take the ring from the velvet box and slide it over her ring finger. Aspen doesn't even bother looking at it, instead she drops to her knees in front of me and wraps her arms around the back of my neck. Cupping her cheeks, I bring her face to mine.

"I love you so much, Aspen. And I can't wait to make you my wife."

"I love you, Cameron," she whispers, a smile forming on her lips as they brush against mine. "I can't wait to be your wife and for our future together."

"Aspen Sawyer," I murmur against her lips, a smile taking over them. "I like the way that sounds."

Aspen laughs softly and I swallow her sounds as I claim her lips with mine. What started out as just a simple arrangement as friends with benefits transformed into something that I never would have imagined happening.

And now that we're here... I can't imagine my life without her.

Without the girl who will soon be my wife.

———

Want more of Cameron and Aspen?
Click here for an exclusive bonus scene!!

———

PROLOGUE

Hayden

Standing by the fire with Sterling and Simon, I slowly sip my beer as they both talk about our hockey game from earlier. It's the summer, so some of the guys went back home to spend the time off from school with their fami-

lies. A few of us stayed back, since we've laid our roots in the small town in Vermont after coming here to play for Wyncote.

The guys who stayed back are all in the summer hockey league to keep up with the demands of meeting our main goal—playing professionally after graduation. In the fall, most of us will be starting our senior year, so we have to stay focused on what we really came here for. The education is above average, but the hockey program at Wyncote is where you want to be.

After my fuck-up last year, coming here was the best move that I could have made. Although I came halfway through the season, I ended up fitting in well with the team and making my place known. I'm exactly where I belong and it helps having three of my childhood friends along my side.

Although, the three of them are practically wifed up now, so you won't see them hanging out at a party like this. Sterling and Simon insisted that I come to the party that Derrick was throwing at the lake. And they were right when they said that it was going to be a rager.

Tuning the two of them out, I see a girl standing across the fire, her eyes narrowed on me. Tilting my head to the side, I raise an eyebrow at her suspiciously. I don't recall ever seeing her anywhere before because she has the type of face that is impossible to erase from your memory.

Staring at her through the flames, my eyes travel across her perfectly symmetrical face. I can't see her eyes clearly, but through the smoke, they look like golden honey. Her hair hangs in perfect waves of amber, hanging down to her waist. She shifts her weight on her feet and my eyes trail down her slim torso and long legs.

The summer's in Vermont get warm and her t-shirt and shorts hug the curves of her body perfectly. She stares back at me with a curious look before looking to the girl beside her as they fall into a conversation. She's a mystery to me and I need to shake the warmth that spreads through my body. I like to indulge in distractions from time to time, but she doesn't look like the type that would just be that.

I drain the rest of my beer before leaving the guys at the fire as I head over to the keg. As I fill up my plastic cup, I chug the light colored liquid before filling it up again. Those light brown eyes drift into my mind and I know that I need to erase them. Especially when she looks like she's fallen from heaven herself.

"You good, man?" Simon asks me as he comes up beside me and fills up his cup too. His eyes are on mine, his eyebrows drawn together in confusion as he watches me chug my beer again.

I nod, wiping the liquid from my mouth with the back of my hand, before holding my cup back to him to refill it. "The heat from the fire was getting to me." And the heated gaze from the other side of the flames.

"I would tell you to go jump in the lake, but maybe not, considering how much you've drank already."

A chuckle vibrates through my chest and I lightly punch him in the arm. "I'm good, bro, but thanks for looking out."

"Sure," he smiles back at me as some girl comes up to him, sliding her arm through his. Simon glances down at her before looking back to me as she tugs on him. "I'll catch up with you later."

Nodding at him, I watch as he walks away with the girl. My eyes scan the shore of the lake, noticing that Sterling's sitting at the fire with some girl on his lap. I'm not surprised, seeing both of them hooking up with some random chicks. Since that seems to be what we do on the regular, unlike August, Logan and Cam. They all ended up in the relationships that we've been trying to avoid.

Stepping away from the keg, I noticed that the gold eyed beauty disappeared. And I don't feel like standing around while Sterling swallows some chick's tongue. Turning my back from them, I head toward the lake, stepping onto the wooden dock as I make my way down to the end of it. The sides are lined with lights and the sound of the water eases my soul as I sit down along the edge.

Hanging my arms over the railing, I sip my beer as I stare out at the dark water, the sounds from the party behind me. Music plays from the speakers set up on the beach, but it doesn't drown out the rippling sounds of the lake against the dock.

"You know, the party is back there," a soft, singsong voice wraps itself around my eardrums. The sound is like silk, like a melody that I could get lost in. A shiver rises up my spine as I crane my neck, glancing over my shoulder.

The girl from earlier steps closer to me, not stopping until she drops down on the dock beside me. "I don't blame you for coming out here. It's peaceful by the water... although you strike me as someone who would prefer chaos instead."

Turning my head to look at her, I raise an eyebrow at her. "Do I know you?"

Her brown eyes are brighter than they appeared at the fire and a ghost of a smile plays on her lips. "Not yet."

My eyes widen slightly, a smirk forming on my face as I stare back at her. She's a goddamn mystery and now she has my fucking attention.

"What's your name?" I ask her, my voice thick with tension as my cock grows in my pants. I can't help myself *as the scent of her perfume—a light vanilla smell—invades my senses.*

She shakes her head at me. "I'm not here to exchange names or numbers with you. I'm here because I need a distraction and you looked like the perfect candidate for a bad decision when I saw you across the fire."

"What do you need a distraction from, pretty girl?" I question her, tilting my head to the side in curiosity. The alcohol is heavy in my system now and I'd be lying if I said that I wasn't drunk. Judging by the glossiness in her gaze, I think she's close to the same level as me.

"Hard pass," she laughs lightly, the sound vibrating against my eardrums. "I'm not here to divulge any of my secrets. I told you what I'm here for."

"You want me to be your bad decision?" My lips curl upward into a sinister smirk as I rise to my feet and extend my hand to her. "I can be whatever you want me to be, baby."

She slides her palm against mine, the warmth spreading up my arm like liquid fire as she wraps her slender fingers around my hand. I pull her to her feet and she stands up in front of me. Tilting my head down, I notice that even though she's got legs for days, she's still a good six inches shorter than me.

Her eyes shine up at me under the moonlight, bouncing back and forth between mine as she narrows them at me. "*Before you start on some gentleman shit, yes I am drunk and yes, I am still sure.*"

Reaching out to her face, I brush a piece of hair away from her face and tuck it behind her ear. Her lips part slightly as I drag my fingertips down the length of her throat, feeling her soft skin shiver under my touch. Dropping my face to hers, my lips lightly brush against hers, our breaths mixing together.

"*Don't worry, baby. I'm not a gentleman.*"

"*Good,*" she breathes, her voice husky as she laces her fingers through mine. "*Come with me.*"

I let her lead me down the dock, back toward the party. As our feet reach the beach, she begins to walk in the opposite direction, taking me with her as we walk through the sand. This isn't the first time that I've had a girl approach me like this. And who am I to say no? I don't have any commitments holding me back.

"*Where are we going?*" I question her, as she leads me towards a clearing that leads through the trees.

She glances over her shoulder at me, mischief dancing in her eyes. "*You'll see.*"

As we walk through the clearing, she leads me down a path to where there's at least a dozen tents set up. I stop in my tracks, confused by the scene laid out in front of me, when it clicks in my drunken mind. Sterling had mentioned that some people were camping here, just so *they didn't have to worry about drinking and driving. I kind of tuned him out when he said that, because I wasn't the one driving here and finding a place to crash was never hard for me.*

She leads me past a few of the tents before she stops by one that's tucked away in the far corner. "This one is mine," she whispers as she unzips the door to the tent and steps inside, pulling me in with her. It's hard to see in the darkness of the night and I trip over something that feels like a duffle bag.

There's an air mattress lying in the center with an open sleeping bag on top of it. I watch her, my heart pounding in my chest as she slowly spins around to face me, her hand leaving mine. We stand in silence for a moment, both of our breathing shallow as our eyes adjust to how we look in the dark. Stepping toward her, my hands reach out for her hips and I jerk her toward me until her body is crashing into mine.

"You sure you want this, babe?" I question her, sliding my hand along the back of her neck as she tilts her head back to look up at me.

"You ask a lot of questions for someone with a playboy reputation, King," she murmurs, my last name rolling off her tongue like that's exactly where it belongs.

And I want to fucking taste it.

CAMERON AND ASPEN
BONUS SCENE

Coming up from the water, I watch Aspen as she swims in the clear water of the ocean. We're nearing the end of our honeymoon trip in Aruba and I'm not ready to go home. As much as I miss Vermont and the life we've built together, I've been enjoying our time together.

Aspen swims over to me, wrapping her arms around the back of my neck. "Hey, husband." She smiles as happiness consumes her face.

"Hey, wife." I smile back at her, pressing my lips to hers. I love seeing Aspen like this—so carefree and happy. She has been super stressed with med school lately, so after our wedding, this getaway was much-needed.

My mind drifts back to the day we got married.

Thinking of our wedding, the way Aspen looked as she walked down the aisle to me. Her white dress trailing behind her, her hair flowing down to the middle of her back. I swear to God, I couldn't breathe with how breathtaking she looked.

"Penny for your thoughts?" she questions me as we float in the ocean together.

I wrap my arms around her waist, pulling her body flush to mine. "Just thinking about our wedding. One of the best days of my life."

Aspen tilts her head to the side. "You mean it wasn't *the* best day of your life?"

"It's a tie between that and the day you agreed to actually tutor me." I smirk, my fingers digging into her flesh. "If you wouldn't have said yes, we might not be here."

"That's true," she says thoughtfully, her eyes burning a hole through mine. "You were extremely persistent and persuasive. It was hard to say no."

I smile at her as she wraps her legs around my waist. "I'm glad I was able to persuade you. Thank God for this charm, it actually came in handy for once."

The lilt of Aspen's laughter slides across my eardrums like silk. "You're crazy, but I love your crazy."

Lifting her in my arms, I walk through the water, carrying her onto the beach. There aren't many people around and she wraps her arms around the back of my neck as I carry her to our private cabana. My thighs hit the side of the mattress and I gently lower her onto it before pulling away.

"What are you up to, Cameron Sawyer?" She smirks as I step over to the curtain and pull it shut.

Turning back to face her, I slide my hands under the waistband of my swim trunks and I push them down. My cock is already hard and Aspen raises an eyebrow at me as I move closer to her. Pushing her legs apart, I climb onto the bed with her, settling between her thighs.

"Checking something off your honeymoon bucket list."

Aspen smiles at me, lifting her back up as I reach around and undo the top of her bathing suit. I toss it onto the bed beside us instead of onto the sand beneath the bed. When we were at the airport, Aspen confessed this little bucket list of things she wanted to do on our honeymoon.

There was only one we hadn't checked off yet.

Having sex in a cabana, in the middle of the day while there are other people on the beach.

"You're bad," she breathes, lifting her hips as I

slide off her bathing suit bottoms. My eyes trail over her sun-kissed skin until I reach her gaze. "Don't stop."

Shifting my body farther down, I slide my arms under her thighs and bury my face in between her legs. Licking her pussy, I slide my tongue along her center, pausing as I reach her clit. Aspen's hands are in my hair as I taste and tease her, rolling the small bundle of nerves with my lips.

Her hips are bucking, fucking my face as I continue to move my tongue around, licking and sucking her. She's silent, but her breathing is rapid and shallow as she grips my hair. She doesn't want anyone to hear us and she's struggling as I push her closer to the edge of ecstasy.

Rolling my tongue across her clit once more, that's all it takes before she's coming on my tongue. She tastes as sweet as she always does and I drink every fucking sip of her. Aspen is a mess, her body twitching and her legs quivering around my head. As I pull away from her, a smile touches my lips as I see her struggling to catch her breath.

Crawling back to her, I settle back between her legs, my cock sliding inside her in one fluid movement. Aspen gasps, her eyes widening as they meet my gaze.

"Oh my god, Cam," she breathes, her voice hoarse and thick with need. "I want you to fuck me hard."

"What if people hear us, baby?" I ask, pressing my lips to hers.

The corners of her lips lift into a smirk. "Then let them hear us."

She wraps her arms around the back of my neck as she wraps her legs around my waist. Sliding one hand behind the back of her head and the other under her ass, our mouths collide as I begin to thrust into her, filling her to the brim.

Aspen moves against me as I continue to fuck her, harder with each thrust. She moans into my mouth and I swallow the sound, our tongues sliding against one another. I lose myself in her, forgetting everything that's going on outside of our cabana. Nothing matters except for the two of us in this moment.

It's so much more than just checking off one of her things from her bucket list. It's the two of us making love, not giving a fuck about the world existing outside of our relationship. And that's exactly how it's meant to be with us.

I pound into her, and my balls constrict as they smack against her ass. I can feel my orgasm building, the warmth spreading through my body before it hits me out of nowhere. I literally don't even see it coming, but as soon as Aspen's pussy clenches, tightening around me, it's game over.

Slamming into her once more, I push both of us over the edge as we fall into the euphoric abyss together. Aspen loses herself around my cock and I lose myself inside her, filling her with my cum. My thrusts begin to slow as we ride out the high from our orgasms. I slowly pull out of her, lifting my mouth from hers.

Collapsing onto the bed beside her, we're both on our sides facing one another. "I love you, Aspen Sawyer," I breathe, brushing a stray hair from her face.

"I love how that sounds, but not as much as I love you."

Scooting closer to her, I wrap my arms around her and pull her to my chest. My beautiful fucking wife. The woman I will love for the rest of my days.

And I can't wait for forever with her.

NEXT IN THE SERIES

The Faceoff is the fourth book from the Wyncote Wolves, featuring Hayden and Eden. Continue reading to the next page for a look inside The Faceoff.

PROLOGUE
HAYDEN

Standing by the fire with Sterling and Simon, I slowly sip my beer as they both talk about our hockey game from earlier. It's the summer, so some of the guys went back home to spend the time off from school with their families. A few of us stayed back, since we've laid our roots in the small town in Vermont after coming here to play for Wyncote.

The guys who stayed back are all in the summer hockey league to keep up with the demands of meeting our main goal—playing professionally after graduation. In the fall, most of us will be starting our senior year, so we have to stay focused on what we really came here for. The education is above average, but the hockey program at Wyncote is where you want to be.

After my fuck-up last year, coming here was the best

move that I could have made. Although I came halfway through the season, I ended up fitting in well with the team and making my place known. I'm exactly where I belong and it helps having three of my childhood friends by my side.

Although, the three of them are practically wifed up now, so you won't see them hanging out at a party like this. Sterling and Simon insisted that I come to the party that Derrick was throwing at the lake. And they were right when they said that it was going to be a rager.

Tuning the two of them out, I see a girl standing across the fire, her eyes narrowed on me. Tilting my head to the side, I raise an eyebrow at her suspiciously. I don't recall ever seeing her anywhere before because she has the type of face that is impossible to erase from your memory.

Staring at her through the flames, my eyes travel across her perfectly symmetrical face. I can't see her eyes clearly, but through the smoke, they look like golden honey. Her hair hangs in perfect waves of amber, hanging down to her waist. She shifts her weight on her feet and my eyes trail down her slim torso and long legs.

The summer's in Vermont get warm and her t-shirt and shorts hug the curves of her body perfectly. She stares back at me with a curious look before looking to the girl beside her as they fall into a conversation. She's a mystery to me and I need to shake the warmth that spreads through my body. I like to indulge in distractions from time to time, but she doesn't look like the type that would just be that.

I drain the rest of my beer before leaving the guys at the fire as I head over to the keg. As I fill up my plastic cup, I chug the light colored liquid before filling it up again. Those light brown eyes drift into my mind and I know that I need to erase them. Especially when she looks like she's fallen from heaven herself.

"You good, man?" Simon asks me as he comes up beside me and fills up his cup too. His eyes are on mine, his eyebrows drawn together in confusion as he watches me chug my beer again.

I nod, wiping the liquid from my mouth with the back of my hand, before holding my cup back to him to refill it. "The heat from the fire was getting to me." And the heated gaze from the other side of the flames.

"I would tell you to go jump in the lake, but maybe not, considering how much you've drank already."

A chuckle vibrates through my chest and I lightly punch him in the arm. "I'm good, bro, but thanks for looking out."

"Sure," he smiles back at me as some girl comes up to him, sliding her arm through his. Simon glances down at

her before looking back to me as she tugs on him. "I'll catch up with you later."

Nodding at him, I watch as he walks away with the girl. My eyes scan the shore of the lake, noticing that Sterling's sitting at the fire with some girl on his lap. I'm not surprised, seeing both of them hooking up with some random chicks. Since that seems to be what we do on the regular, unlike August, Logan and Cam. They all ended up in the relationships that we've been trying to avoid.

Stepping away from the keg, I noticed that the gold eyed beauty disappeared. And I don't feel like standing around while Sterling swallows some chick's tongue. Turning my back from them, I head toward the lake, stepping onto the wooden dock as I make my way down to the end of it. The sides are lined with lights and the sound of the water eases my soul as I sit down along the edge.

Hanging my arms over the railing, I sip my beer as I stare out at the dark water, the sounds from the party behind me. Music plays from the speakers set up on the beach, but it doesn't drown out the rippling sounds of the lake against the dock.

"You know, the party is back there," a soft, singsong voice wraps itself around my eardrums. The sound is like silk, like a melody that I could get lost in. A shiver rises

up my spine as I crane my neck, glancing over my shoulder.

The girl from earlier steps closer to me, not stopping until she drops down on the dock beside me. "I don't blame you for coming out here. It's peaceful by the water... although you strike me as someone who would prefer chaos instead."

Turning my head to look at her, I raise an eyebrow at her. "Do I know you?"

Her brown eyes are brighter than they appeared at the fire and a ghost of a smile plays on her lips. "Not yet."

My eyes widen slightly, a smirk forming on my face as I stare back at her. She's a goddamn mystery and now she has my fucking attention.

"What's your name?" I ask her, my voice thick with tension as my cock grows in my pants. I can't help myself as the scent of her perfume—a light vanilla smell— invades my senses.

She shakes her head at me. "I'm not here to exchange names or numbers with you. I'm here because I need a distraction and you looked like the perfect candidate for a bad decision when I saw you across the fire."

"What do you need a distraction from, pretty girl?" I question her, tilting my head to the side in curiosity. The alcohol is heavy in my system now and I'd be lying if I said that I wasn't drunk. Judging by the glossiness in her gaze, I think she's close to the same level as me.

"Hard pass," she laughs lightly, the sound vibrating against my eardrums. "I'm not here to divulge any of my secrets. I told you what I'm here for."

"You want me to be your bad decision?" My lips curl upward into a sinister smirk as I rise to my feet and extend my hand to her. "I can be whatever you want me to be, baby."

She slides her palm against mine, the warmth spreading up my arm like liquid fire as she wraps her slender fingers around my hand. I pull her to her feet and she stands up in front of me. Tilting my head down, I notice that even though she's got legs for days, she's still a good six inches shorter than me.

Her eyes shine up at me under the moonlight, bouncing back and forth between mine as she narrows them at me. "Before you start on some gentleman shit, yes I am drunk and yes, I am still sure."

Reaching out to her face, I brush a piece of hair away from her face and tuck it behind her ear. Her lips part slightly as I drag my fingertips down the length of her throat, feeling her soft skin shiver under my touch. Dropping my face to hers, my lips lightly brush against hers, our breaths mixing together.

"Don't worry, baby. I'm not a gentleman."

"Good," she breathes, her voice husky as she laces her fingers through mine. "Come with me."

I let her lead me down the dock, back toward the party. As our feet reach the beach, she begins to walk in the opposite direction, taking me with her as we walk through the sand. This isn't the first time that I've had a girl approach me like this. And who am I to say no? I don't have any commitments holding me back.

"Where are we going?" I question her, as she leads me towards a clearing the leads through the trees.

She glances over her shoulder at me, mischief dancing in her eyes. "You'll see."

As we walk through the clearing, she leads me down a path to where there's at least a dozen tents set up. I stop in my tracks, confused by the scene laid out in front of me, when it clicks in my drunken mind. Sterling had mentioned that some people were camping here, just so they didn't have to worry about drinking and driving. I kind of tuned him out when he said that, because I wasn't the one driving here and finding a place to crash was never hard for me.

She leads me past a few of the tents before she stops by one that's tucked away in the far corner. "This one is mine," she whispers as she unzips the door to the tent and steps inside, pulling me in with her. It's hard to see *in the darkness of the night and I trip over something that feels like a duffle bag.*

There's an air mattress lying in the center with an open sleeping bag on top of it. I watch her, my heart pounding in my chest as she slowly spins around to face me, her hand leaving mine. We stand in silence for a moment, both of our breathing shallow as our eyes adjust to how we look in the dark. Stepping toward her, my hands reach out for her hips and I jerk her toward me until her body is crashing into mine.

"You sure you want this, babe?" I question her, sliding my hand along the back of her neck as she tilts her head back to look up at me.

"You ask a lot of questions for someone with a playboy reputation, King," she murmurs, my last name rolling off her tongue like that's exactly where it belongs.

And I want to fucking taste it.

ALSO BY CALI MELLE

WYNCOTE WOLVES SERIES

Cross Checked Hearts

Deflected Hearts

Playing Offsides

The Faceoff

The Goalie Who Stole Christmas

ABOUT THE AUTHOR

Cali Melle is a contemporary romance author who loves writing stories that will pull at your heartstrings. You can always expect her stories to come fully equipped with heartthrobs and a happy ending, along with some steamy scenes and some sports action. In her free time, Cali can usually be found spending time with her family or with her nose in a book. As a hockey and figure skating mom, you can probably find her freezing at a rink while watching her kids chase their dreams.

Printed in Great Britain
by Amazon

12736035R00174